24-9-20

0-11-

Thi:
late:
perio:

- P
- Vi:

THE MAN
EVERY WOMAN
WANTS

THE MAN EVERY WOMAN WANTS

BY

MIRANDA LEE

MILLS
BOON®

First published in Great Britain 2011
by Mills & Boon, an imprint of Harlequin (UK) Limited.
Large Print edition 2012
Harlequin (UK) Limited, Eton House,
18-24 Paradise Road, Richmond, Surrey TW9 1SR

© Miranda Lee 2011

ISBN: 978 0 263 22567 9

Printed and bound in Great Britain
by CPI Antony Rowe, Chippenham, Wiltshire

CHAPTER ONE

RYAN Armstrong never mixed business with pleasure.

His was very much a case of once bitten, a zillion times shy. Not that the word 'shy' fitted Ryan's confident and outgoing personality. So cross out 'shy' and put 'wary' instead.

Ryan was wary of the complications and consequences which came from mixing business and pleasure. *Very* wary.

When he'd been younger and not involved in the business world there'd been no need to resist temptation when it had come to the fairer sex. If he'd been attracted to a girl, he'd never stopped to think before his male hormones had sent him off in pursuit. He was usually successful in that pursuit, Mother Nature having endowed him with the sort of tall, broad-shouldered and extremely athletic body which women lusted after and which had seen him rise to become one of the world's most successful and well-paid goalkeepers. From the ages of twenty-three to twenty-nine, during which he'd played international soccer for several European clubs, he'd had more girlfriends than he'd saved goals.

When injury had forced early retirement at the age of thirty, and he had set up his own sports-management company back in Sydney, Ryan unfortunately had not developed the good habit of either controlling or ignoring his sexual urges. So when one of his first female clients—who was very attractive as well as a great athlete—started flirting with Ryan, it was inevitable that they would end up in bed together. Given she was nearly thirty and totally dedicated to her sports career, Ryan never imagined that she would want anything more from him than a casual fling.

By the end of their second date, however, Ryan had seen that he'd made a huge mistake. The girl had constantly sent him text messages raving about his love-making abilities, then saying how much she was going to enjoy being his wife. When he'd tried to finish things—very tactfully, he'd thought—she had gone all out to destroy his business. She'd released confidential information to the papers, plus had tried to drag his name through the mud in every possible way.

Unfortunately, by then he'd deleted all those revealing messages and it had been a case of her word against his. He'd come out the winner in the end, but it had been a close call. Ryan shuddered whenever he thought how close he'd come to losing everything he'd worked for. His business had still suffered for a while, hence his rule about mixing business with pleasure.

These days, he only dated mature, sensible women who had absolutely nothing to do with the Win-Win Sports Management Agency. He steered well clear of female clients and employees. He even trod carefully when it came to any kind of close business-colleague. His current girlfriend was a public-relations executive from a firm whose services he never used. Erica was blonde, thirty-five years old, divorced, childless and ruthlessly ambitious.

Thankfully, she was no more interested in marriage than he was. Or falling in love, for that matter. She'd been there, done that and it hadn't worked out. She suited Ryan's needs admirably, being attractive, intelligent and sexy. Ryan had discovered over the last few years that driven career-girls were usually hot between the sheets—and not given to huge tantrums when he wanted to move on.

Ryan moved on every few months. Occasionally, a relationship would last a little longer, but usually not. Often they ended earlier, once or twice after only a few weeks. Ryan always opted out very quickly if he thought he was becoming involved with a potential problem. He'd reached an age—he would turn thirty-eight next birthday—by which most guys had given up their bachelor days in favour of marriage and a family. He'd seen it happen time and time again. All his male friends were now married, even the ones whom he'd thought would never succumb to the urge to settle down and have children.

Ryan could well understand why members of the opposite sex saw him as a suitable target for marriage. Because he never talked about his past, what they didn't know was that he'd decided a long time ago that he would never become a husband and father. And he hadn't changed his mind about that.

A sharp tap-tap on the office door interrupted his thoughts and sent his eyes to the clock on his desk. Exactly three p.m.; right on time as usual, Ryan thought with illogical irritation. He actually admired punctuality. He hated wasting time waiting for people, especially when he'd made an appointment. So why didn't he admire it at three p.m. every Friday afternoon?

'Come in, Laura,' he called out through clenched teeth.

She came in, looking exactly the same as she always looked: severely tailored black suit with black hair up in an equally severe French pleat. No make-up. No jewellery. No perfume.

As she crossed the room towards the chair she always occupied during their weekly meeting, Ryan looked her up and down and wondered why she did that to herself. Did she imagine that this was how a female lawyer should look—tough, hard, and totally sexless?

Anyone could see that she could be a very attractive woman if she tried. She had a good figure and an interesting face with high cheekbones and exotically shaped grey eyes. Admittedly, those eyes were usually as cold as an arctic sky, especially when they looked at him.

So Ryan was startled when their eyes met and he glimpsed not chilly indifference for once but a type of pained regret. She even stopped walking for a second to stare at him.

'What?' he said straight away.

'Nothing,' she replied, and shook her head.

'Sorry. Let's get straight down to business, shall we?' She sat down, crossed her legs with her usual crisp modesty then leant forward to pick up the first of the contracts which were sitting on the edge of his desk waiting for her perusal.

It was a lucrative endorsement deal he'd personally negotiated for an up-and-coming young male tennis-player whom Win-Win had been lucky enough to sign up the previous month. A lot of Ryan's work involved negotiating contracts of one sort or another, all of which he always had checked over by one of the best legal brains in the whole of Sydney—which Laura had.

She wasn't an employee of Win-Win; Ryan didn't need a lawyer to work for him full-time. His company was more of the boutique variety. She worked for Harvey, Michaels and Associates, an American-owned legal firm with a Sydney branch which was conveniently located in the same building as Ryan's business and which boasted a stable of brilliant criminal and corporate lawyers.

When Ryan had become one of their clients several years ago, they had originally sent him a young male lawyer at Ryan's request—a smart guy, but a very bad driver who'd wrapped his car around a tree two years back. When the firm had suggested a female replacement, Ryan had been hesitant at first, especially when he had found out she was only thirty and single. But as soon as he had met Laura Ryan had realised there was no chance of his becoming involved with her. Or vice versa.

She still wasn't a problem in that regard. But she could be irritating all the same. Ryan wasn't used to being treated with such patent indifference by members of the opposite sex. It irked his male ego, which was considerable. Sometimes her disinterest seemed to border on outright dislike. It crossed his mind occasionally that she might not be interested in men, but he had no real evidence of this. It seemed more likely that past experiences had turned her into a man-hater—either that or she'd never met a man capable of melting her frozen exterior.

Once, a couple of weeks ago when she'd been particularly frosty with him, he'd been taken by the sudden urge to pull her into his arms and kiss her silly, just to see if he could get a reaction out of her.

He hadn't given in to that urge, of course. Ryan knew if he did any such thing he'd have a world of trouble on his hands faster than a world-class striker could score a goal—amazingly fast.

Besides, he had a lot more control over his testosterone these days. On the surface, that was. His mind, however, had given way to fantasies about the infernal woman all that afternoon.

A wry smile curved his lips as he recalled what he'd done to her in his head, and how avidly she'd responded.

In your dreams, Ryan!

'What's so funny?'

Ryan's head snapped clear at her caustic question, his amusement replaced by surprise. It wasn't like Laura to notice anything when she was reading through a contract. She almost never glanced up until she was finished, which she obviously wasn't. By the look of things, she'd only reached the second page of the five-page document.

'Nothing to do with you, Laura,' he lied. 'Just looking forward to the weekend. I'm going sailing with some friends tomorrow.' Which he was. Erica was away this weekend in Melbourne, attending a conference.

Laura's sigh also surprised him. It sounded… envious.

'Lucky you.'

'Want to come?' The invitation was out of his mouth before he could snatch it back.

She blinked with shock before dropping her eyes back to the contract. 'Sorry,' she said brusquely. 'I'm busy this weekend.'

Wow, he thought. That was a narrow escape. Whatever had possessed him to invite her? Still, his ego was slightly stroked by her not having said no outright. Maybe she wasn't as indifferent to his charms as she always seemed.

Ryan knew most women were attracted to him, as they were to most tall, good-looking, successful men.

No false modesty about Ryan.

He didn't interrupt her as she finished reading the contract but his mind remained extremely active. So did his eyes.

She really did have great legs. He liked women with shapely calves and slender ankles, and feet which weren't too big. Laura's feet were quite daintily small for a girl of her height. Pity about those awful shoes she was wearing!

Her hair was great too: dark, thick, glossy and obviously long. It would look fabulous spread out against a pillow...

Whoops. He was doing it again: having sexual fantasies about her. He really had to stop this.

Swinging his chair round to the huge window behind him, Ryan stared out at the view of the harbour which he always found pleasurably diverting and was one of the reasons he'd rented this particular suite of rooms in this building. The other reason was that it was less than two blocks from where he lived in an apartment building which also had a wonderful view of the harbour.

When Ryan had first retired from soccer, he'd missed spending most of his life outdoors. He hated the feeling of being closed in. He liked space around him, liked to see the sky—and water, he'd discovered to his surprise. He hadn't grown up with a love of water, mostly because it hadn't been a part of his life; he had never even been taken to the beach as a child. He hadn't learned to swim till he was twenty, and that had only happened because he'd been forced to train in a pool for a few weeks whilst he recovered from injury.

After his return to live in Sydney, however, he had found himself very drawn to the water, hence his buying an apartment and leasing an office that both came with harbour views. Recently, he'd developed a real love of sailing, and was considering buying a boat.

There were plenty of boats out on the harbour that afternoon, winter having finally given way to spring. The rain which had plagued Sydney for the past two months was thankfully gone; the sky was clear and blue and the water inviting.

His eyes zeroed in on one of the boats which was just moving past Bennelong Point, heading out to sea. It was a large white cruiser, an expensive toy for someone with plenty of money.

Maybe I'll buy one of those, Ryan thought idly.

He could well afford it; Win-Win wasn't Ryan's only source of income. Back during his goalkeeping days, he'd had the sense to invest most of the huge salary he'd earned each year into property. By the time he had retired, he was the owner of a dozen or so units, all located in Sydney's inner-city suburbs where the rental returns were excellent and the apartments never empty for long.

His extensive property portfolio was another thing Ryan didn't talk about, however, knowing it wasn't wise to broadcast one's wealth. Hc'd found it didn't do to court envy. He had a small group of friends who were successful men in their own right, though not multi-millionaires like him. He enjoyed their company and was loath to do anything to spoil their friendship. Of course, now that they'd all tied the knot, he didn't have quite as much to do with them as he used to. But they still got together occasionally to go to the football or the races.

None of them owned a boat. The 'friends' Ryan was going sailing with tomorrow were not real friends. They were professional yachtsmen whom he'd met through his job and who'd been teaching him the ropes about sailing.

'I can't seem to find anything wrong with it,' Laura said at last, in a troubled tone which suggested she should have been able to.

Ryan swung his chair back round to face her.

'You're quite sure?' he asked. It wasn't like Laura not to want him to change something. She often spotted potential legal loopholes which weren't to his client's advantage.

'Maybe I should read through it again.'

Ryan was as surprised by her suggesting this as he'd been by the odd look she'd given him earlier. Really, she wasn't herself today. Now that he'd stopped filling his mind with distracting images, he could see that *she* was the one who was distracted.

What was it that had upset her so much that her mind wasn't on her work? It had to be something serious.

A curious Ryan decided to see if he could find out.

'No need to do that,' he said. 'I'm sure it's fine. Why don't you have a quick whizz through the other two contracts? They're just renewals. Then we'll call it a day and I'll take you down to the Opera Bar for a drink.' If he could get her to relax, she might open up to him a bit.

She surprised him again by not saying no straight away.

Curiouser and curiouser.

But she didn't say yes, either.

'Look,' he said firmly. 'I'm not asking you out on a date. Just for a drink. Lots of work colleagues go for drinks on a Friday afternoon.'

'I do know that,' she said stiffly.

'Then what's your problem?'

Again, she hesitated.

'Look,' he went on determinedly, 'I do realise that you don't like me much. No no, Laura, don't bother to deny it; you've made your feelings quite obvious over the past two years. I have to confess that I haven't exactly warmed to you, either.

But even the most indifferent and insensitive male would notice that you're not yourself today. As unlikely as it might seem, I find myself quite worried about you. Hence my invitation to take you for a drink. I thought you might relax over a glass of wine and tell me what's up.'

And why you gave me that odd look when you first came in, he added privately to himself.

'Even if I tell you,' she replied, her eyes unhappy, 'There's nothing *you* can do about it.'

'Let me be the judge of that.'

She laughed, but it was not a happy sound. 'You'll probably be annoyed with me.'

'That's a very intriguing thing to say. Now, I simply won't take no for an answer. You are going to come for a drink with me—right now. And you're going to tell me what this is all about!'

CHAPTER TWO

LAURA knew it was silly of her to feel flattered by his concern—and even sillier to agree to have a drink with him at the Opera Bar, of all places.

The Opera Bar was *the* place to go for an after-work drink in Sydney's CBD, conveniently located near the quay and with one of the best views in town—the Opera House on the right, Circular Quay on the left, the Harbour Bridge straight ahead, not to mention the harbour itself. Half the staff at Harvey, Michaels and Associates gathered there every Friday evening. Even non-social Laura occasionally went with them. She knew that it would cause a stir if she was seen drinking there in the company of Ryan Armstrong.

Why, then, had she agreed?

This was the question which tormented her during the short walk down to the quay.

By the time they arrived at the bar—early enough not to be spotted by any of her work colleagues yet, thank heavens—Laura was no nearer a logical answer.

Alison would have said that she was secretly attracted to him. There again, dear Alison was a hopeless romantic, addicted to those movies where the heroine hates the hero on sight but somehow falls madly in love with him before the credits go up at the end.

Laura could never buy into that plot. When she didn't like someone, she didn't like them—end of story. She'd never liked Ryan Armstrong and certainly wasn't secretly attracted to him.

Okay, so he was good-looking, smart and, yes, highly successful. Ten years ago, she might have found him fascinating. These days, however, she was immune to handsome charmers who used women for their sexual satisfaction—sometimes for other rotten reasons—and gave them nothing in return but the dubious pleasure of their company. They shared nothing of themselves, either emotionally or financially. They were greedy selfish men who wanted their cake and wanted to eat it too. Laura had been involved with two such men in her life and had developed a sixth sense whenever she met a man of their ilk.

Ryan Armstrong had set off warning bells in her

head from the first moment they had met, which was why she made an extra effort every Friday to down-play her looks even more than had become her habit during the last few years.

Not that she needed to worry about his making a play for her. It had been obvious from the start that he didn't like her any more than she liked him. That was why she'd been surprised today by his suddenly being nice to her. He'd got under her guard a couple of times already and now here she was, about to have drinks with him.

It was all very perverse.

'Let's sit outside,' Ryan said, and steered her out to the alfresco area where the sun was still shining, providing enough warmth to counter the freshness of the harbour breeze.

'What would you like to drink?' Ryan asked as he pulled out a chair for her at an empty table right by the water's edge.

'Bourbon and coke,' she replied, which made him raise his eyebrows. But he made no verbal comment before turning away and returning to the bar inside to order the drinks.

Being left alone gave Laura even more time to think and to worry. Not about her virtue—no way could she ever be seduced by the likes of Ryan

Armstrong—but about the confession which Ryan was seemingly intent on getting out of her.

She still could not believe she'd been stupid enough to do what she'd done. And now it had backfired on her, big time. Not that she could have foretold that the doctors would be proved wrong and that her grandmother would come out of her coma and remember every single word that her granddaughter had said as she had sat by her bedside. Laura's intentions at the time had all been good, but what did that matter now?

A weary sigh escaped her lips. What was that old saying? 'The road to hell was paved with good intentions.'

The sight of Ryan walking towards their table with the drinks in his hands reminded her of why she'd chosen *him* to lie about to her grandmother. He really was the epitome of what her grandmother would think the perfect partner for her favourite granddaughter. First there was the matter of his looks. Gran had always said that she liked a man to look like a man, advising Laura to steer clear of pretty boys whom, she'd said, invariably had no backbone and, more importantly, no muscles to speak of.

'And they usually go bald early,' Gran had claimed with a perfectly straight face.

Laura had never been overly impressed by her grandmother's tendency to make superficial judgements when it came to the opposite sex. Though perhaps she should have listened, since the two men who'd broken her heart had both been pretty boys.

Ryan certainly wasn't a pretty boy. All his facial features were large and masculine. He had a broad forehead, an aquiline nose and a strong, square jaw which wasn't softened at all by the dimple in the middle of his chin. His hair was dark brown and would have been thick, if he ever grew it past his military-style crew cut. He certainly wasn't in danger of going prematurely bald, with no sign of a receding hairline.

Gran also liked men with blue eyes, for some reason.

Ryan's eyes were blue, though they were so deep-set under his thick dark brows that they sometimes looked black from a distance. Up close, however, their blue was the colour of a bright summer sky—but not nearly as warm. His eyes carried a hardness which no doubt served him well when he was negotiating a deal.

His body would have gained Gran's tick of approval as well, being tall and broad-shouldered, with muscles in all the right places. Admittedly, Laura had never seen him dressed in anything but a business suit—the kind he was wearing today— but she had seen him jacket-less with his sleeves rolled up and there was no hiding the fact that the man was very fit, with a flat stomach and no flab anywhere.

It was no wonder that she'd chosen him as her imaginary Mr Right, she realised as she watched Ryan walk towards her. He fitted the bill perfectly. Not only did he look like a man physically, but he was financially secure, charming when he wanted to be and, yes, old enough to be experienced in life.

Gran always said that a girl should never marry a man around her own age.

'Boys mature much later than girls, Laura,' she'd advised her granddaughter on more than one occasion. 'They need to experience life before they're ready to settle down.'

Of course, when she'd been waxing lyrical about Ryan by her Gran's hospital bed, she hadn't mentioned just how 'experienced' he was, Laura thought caustically. She didn't think her rather old-fashioned grandmother would approve of a man who'd had more women than underpants. And who changed them just as often.

Frankly, it always amazed Laura why women kept getting sucked into having a relationship with Ryan Armstrong. If you could call what he had with women 'relationships'. They were just ships passing in the night from what she'd heard. And she'd heard plenty over the past two years.

He smiled as he placed the drinks down on the table, a wickedly sexy smile which gave her a glimpse of how dangerously attractive he could be. If one was susceptible to that kind of thing.

'I decided to have what you're having,' he said as he sat down and swept up his own bourbon and coke. 'Cheers!'

She picked up her drink, clinked it against his, then took a deep swallow. Their eyes met over the rims of their glasses. His glittered with wry amusement whilst she kept hers as cool as always. But, underneath the silk lining of her black jacket, Laura was startled to feel her heart beating a little faster.

Maybe she wasn't as immune to the man's charms as she imagined. But it was not enough to worry about.

Nevertheless, she glanced away at the harbour. It really was a spectacular setting for a city, especially on a warm spring afternoon. Lots of boats were out on the sparkling water, creating a visual feast for all the tourists who'd flocked to the quayside area to take holiday snaps of the bridge and the Opera House.

'Sydney's a truly beautiful city, isn't it?' Laura said with pride in her voice.

'It surely is,' he agreed. 'You only have to live in other cities in other countries to know how lucky we are.'

She looked back at him. 'You sound like you've lived in lots of other countries.'

Ryan shrugged. 'Quite a few. But no more prevaricating, now,' he said as he put down his glass. 'Tell me what's going on in your life which has sent you into such a spin today.'

'I'm not in a spin,' she said defensively.

'Laura, you're sitting here having a drink with me. That's evidence enough that something has thrown you for a loop. So stop denying it. Given you're not the sort of girl to make a professional mistake, it has to be a personal problem. And I'm involved in some weird way. Am I right about that?'

'Yes,' she said, seeing no point in lying. It was obvious Ryan wasn't going to let up until he knew every depressing detail, so she took a deep breath then launched into her tale of woe.

'It's a bit of a long story, so please be patient with me.'

Patience, she knew, was not one of Ryan's strong points. But he didn't say a word, the expression on his face showing genuine interest. He might feel differently when he learned the part he'd played in her disaster, albeit unknowingly.

'Two weeks ago, my grandmother had a bad fall down some steps and ended up in a coma in hospital. Not in a Sydney hospital— In John Hunter Hospital in Newcastle. Gran lives up in the Hunter Valley. Anyway, the family was told she wasn't likely to pull through. In fact, the doctors didn't even expect her to last the night. So I sat with her all that night and, because I didn't want to go to sleep and not be with her if and when she did pass away, I kept talking to her. And, because I thought it wouldn't matter, I told her all the things that I knew she'd always wanted to hear: that I'd finally found Mr Right and I was very, very happy.

'Of course, it didn't take very long to make that simple announcement, so I was forced to elaborate somewhat to fill in time. Unfortunately, I've never had a great imagination; creativity is not a talent of mine. So I thought of all the men I knew and worked with and came up with the one who fitted the bill of Mr Right from my grandmother's viewpoint. Superficially, that is,' she added with a rueful glance Ryan's way.

'Good God,' he said, sitting up straight. 'You're talking about me, aren't you?'

'Unfortunately, yes,' she admitted dryly.

He laughed, then laughed again. 'Damn it, but that is funny, Laura. In an ironic way,' he added. 'I don't think what happened to your poor grandmother is funny. I have a soft spot for grandmothers.'

Indeed, his eyes did soften with his words.

'I must be missing something here,' he went on, his forehead crinkling into a frown. 'What harm did it do for you to invent a fictitious Mr Right on your grandmother's deathbed? Frankly, I think it was rather sweet of you to do what you did.'

Laura sighed. 'Sweet, but stupid. I should have known that Gran would pull through. She's always been a fighter. Not only did she pull through, but somehow she remembered every single word I said when she was supposed to be unconscious. Well, perhaps that's a slight exaggeration. But she did remember my saying that I'd finally met Mr Right and his name was Ryan Armstrong. Now she's out of hospital and wants me to bring you home to meet her this very weekend.'

'Naturally,' Ryan said, then laughed again.

'Don't laugh—it really isn't funny, because she's still not at all well. The doctors found out that she'd had a small stroke, and that was probably why she fell. The family's been warned that she could have another stroke at any time. Or even a heart attack. They did lots of tests whilst she was in hospital and things are not good, artery-wise; there are a few serious blockages. But she refuses to have a bypass or any kind of invasive treatment. Says she's had a good life and is quite happy to go.'

'Oh dear,' Ryan said with some genuine sympathy in his voice. 'You really have landed yourself in a right pickle, haven't you?'

'I really have. But it's not your problem. I only told you because you insisted.'

'So what are you going to do?'

'I guess I'll delay things for as long as I can. I'll make up some excuse for why you can't come to meet her this weekend—a business trip, or an illness. But I can hardly keep on saying that. In the end, I'll have to tell her the truth—though I don't want to say that I lied about our relationship. She'd be so disappointed with me. I'll have to say that things just didn't work out between us after all.'

'You can say that I didn't want to marry you. Which is true, after all,' he added, smiling.

'Very funny.'

'It is, rather, if you stop to think about it. I can't imagine two more unlikely lovers.'

'Well Gran doesn't know that, does she?' Laura snapped, piqued by his remark.

'No, she doesn't. Of course, there is one other solution to your problem.'

'I can't imagine what.'

'Of course you can't. You don't have an imagination.'

Laura rolled her eyes at him. 'Then enlighten me, oh brilliant one.'

'I could go with you to your grandmother's place this weekend and pretend to be your Mr Right.'

Laura almost spilled the rest of her drink, but she soon gathered her usual poise and gave Ryan the drollest look. 'And why, pray tell, would you do something as sweetly generous, but as patently ridiculous, as that?'

CHAPTER THREE

WHY indeed? Ryan wondered as he quaffed back a good portion of his drink.

He suspected it was because the idea amused the hell out of him. He rather fancied the prospect of Laura having to act the part of his doting girl-friend.

But of course he could hardly say that. And there *was* another reason, one which might convince the surprisingly sentimental Laura into going along with his suggestion.

'As I mentioned before,' he said, 'I have a soft spot for grandmothers. Mine was marvellous to me. I don't know what I would have done without her.' He certainly wouldn't have gone on to be a success in life. She was the one who had first taken him to soccer—even though he was a little old at thirteen to take up the sport, which was why he ended up a goal-keeper. And she was the one who had made him believe that he could put the past behind him and become anything he wanted to be.

'I've always regretted that she died before I could give her all the good things she deserved in life,' he added. More than regret—remorse was more like it. He hadn't realised until she was gone just how much she'd done for him, and how much she meant to him. He'd cried buckets when he found out she'd died, though not in front of any of his teammates. He'd been a very selfish twenty-two at the time and had just been signed to his first contract with a premier league English team. He hadn't returned to Australia for his grandmother's funeral, another deep regret.

He'd been touched by Laura sitting with her grandmother all night, not wanting to leave her to die alone. Clearly, the old lady meant a lot to her.

'It's obvious that you're very close to your grandmother,' he said.

'I am,' Laura said, her voice sounding a little choked up. 'She raised me after my parents were killed in a plane crash.'

'I see…' And he did see. His grandmother had raised him after his own mother had died.

Damn it all, but he didn't want to think about *that*!

'So what do you say to my suggestion?' he asked,

not feeling quite so amused any more. But it was too late to retract his offer.

Laura's expressive eyes showed considerable reserve. 'I have to confess that I'm tempted. But I'm not sure we could bring it off—pretending to be lovers, that is. I mean, we don't even like each other.'

'True,' he said bluntly.

'You don't have to agree with me so readily,' she snapped. 'What is it, exactly, that you don't like about me?'

He smiled. 'You don't really want me to tell you that, do you?'

'I certainly do.'

'Okay, you asked for it. First there's your appearance.'

'There's nothing wrong with my appearance!'

Ryan raised an eyebrow sardonically and infuriatingly she felt herself blush. He continued, 'Then there's your manner.'

'What's wrong with my manner?'

'Well, "ice queen" would be an understatement. Of course,' he went on, unbowed in the face of her outrage, 'If I could persuade you to let your hair down in more ways than one, then it'd be a breeze. Do you think you could do that?'

'I'm not going to tart myself up for the likes of you, Ryan Armstrong,' Laura pronounced huffily.

'And there we have the main reason that I don't like you: because *you* don't like *me*.'

'No,' she bit out. 'I don't.'

'Why not?'

'You don't really want me to tell you that, do you?'

He chuckled. She might not have an imagination but she did have a sharp wit. 'Actually, I'm not so sure that I don't like you,' he said. 'You are very amusing company.'

She made no comment, just gave him another of her dry looks.

'Do you have a boyfriend, Laura?' he asked abruptly.

'Don't be ridiculous,' she retorted. 'If I had a boyfriend do you think I would be in this damned awful predicament?'

'Having a boyfriend does not equate with your finding Mr Right. But let me rephrase that—are you sleeping with anyone at the moment?'

Her eyes grew even colder, if that were possible.

'I'm between boyfriends at the moment,' she said tartly.

'Ah.'

'And what does that mean?' she demanded to know.

'Ah just means ah.'

'I very much doubt that. You think I'm not capable of getting a boyfriend, don't you? You think I'm too cold.'

Wow, he thought, how right you are. But rather fascinatingly frosty. What he wouldn't give to have the chance to melt some of that ice. Unfortunately, a man could get frostbite trying.

He'd have to watch himself with her this weekend.

'What I think,' he said after careful consideration, 'Is that you've been hurt by some man in your past which has given you a jaundiced view of the male sex.'

The slight widening of her eyes showed him he was on the right track with his analysis of her character.

'Lots of attractive women who've been badly treated by men subconsciously do things to make themselves less attractive so that they won't be hit on. Some change their appearance by putting on weight. Some dress in a manner which hides their femininity. Which I think—'

The sound of his phone ringing interrupted his spiel.

'Excuse me,' he said to Laura as he fished the phone out of his jacket pocket and glanced at the identity of the caller.

Damn. It was Erica.

CHAPTER FOUR

LAURA welcomed the interruption. Ryan's interpretation of her character was too close to the bone for her liking. Because of course he was right. Subconsciously, she knew why she dressed the way she did and acted the way she did. But no man had said as much to her out loud before.

She didn't like it. It made her feel vulnerable and weak. A coward, even. Yet she wasn't a coward—*was* she?

The thought tormented her. Alison was always saying that she should give the male sex another chance. But then what would Alison know? She was married to a great guy who was loving and loyal and would never hurt her. She'd never known what it felt like to have one's heart ripped out, not just by one man, but two. Laura knew she couldn't afford to open herself to hurt of that kind ever again because if she did, and disaster struck a third time, she suspected she would not survive.

Admittedly, sometimes she was very lonely.

Sometimes, she wished her life had been different; if only she'd found someone decent when she'd been younger and still full of hope. Life's experiences, however, had finally turned her into a hard-hearted cynic, but quite a good judge of character. Nowadays, when she met an attractive man, she quickly saw through his looks to the man beneath.

She knew exactly what sort of man Ryan Armstrong was: the sort who would break a girl's heart and never lose a moment's sleep over it.

But he was not totally bad, she accepted as she glanced over the rim of her glass at him. Clearly he was capable of kindness.

'Hi,' he said into his phone. 'How's things going?'

He'd turned his body away from the table to answer the phone but Laura could still hear him clearly enough. The bar was beginning to fill up but the noise wasn't too bad, and the music hadn't yet started.

'That boring, huh?' he went on. 'No, I'm down at the Opera Bar having a drink with a friend from work.'

Laura frowned, knowing instantly that Ryan was being evasive to whomever he was talking to on the phone. His girlfriend, perhaps? He was sure to have one. He always had some girl on tap from what she'd heard. She'd forgotten about that when he'd offered to pretend to be her Mr Right this weekend.

What on earth did he plan to tell the girlfriend if she agreed to his suggestion? Laura couldn't imagine any female enjoying their boyfriend pretending to be another woman's boyfriend, no matter how innocent it really was.

'I'll ring you later tonight, sweetheart,' she heard him saying, confirming her suspicion that he was talking to his current girlfriend. 'Bye for now.'

He hung up and swung back to face her. 'Now, where was I?' he said as he put his phone away.

Laura decided to put a spanner in his works with some much-needed honesty.

'Your girlfriend wouldn't like you pretending to be my Mr Right,' she said with chilly disdain in her voice. 'Or were you thinking about not telling her?'

His eyes grew even colder than her own, if that were possible. 'Erica does not own me, Laura. Besides, she's in Melbourne this weekend for a conference.'

'You mean what she doesn't know doesn't hurt her?'

'Actually, I have every intention of telling Erica when I ring her back later tonight.'

'Really.' Laura could not keep the sarcasm out of her voice. In her experience, lying to their girl-friends was second nature to men like Ryan.

'Yes, really. But I can see you don't believe me.'

'Does it matter what I believe? It's all irrelevant anyway, because I've decided not to accept your kind offer.'

'And why's that?'

'Because it can only lead to further complica-tions. Gran's eightieth birthday is coming up soon. If her health improves, the family is sure to throw her a party and she'll expect me to attend, along with my newly found Mr Right. I can't honestly expect you to go along to that as well. By then, we'll be asked eternal questions about when we're getting engaged and when the wedding's going to be. Everything will snowball and you'll wish you hadn't started it in the first place. Much better I go home this weekend and say we've already broken up.'

Ryan shrugged. 'If that's what you want to do. But it wouldn't worry Erica.'

'If you think that, Ryan, then you don't know women very well. I think I should go now,' she added, becoming nervous that people from her work would start arriving any minute now. 'Thank you for the drink, and for your offer. It really was very nice of you. But not a good idea.'

She finished her drink and stood up. 'I'll see you next Friday at three,' she said.

'I tell you what,' Ryan said before she could escape. 'I'll give you my private mobile-number just in case you change your mind. Do you have a biro in that bag of yours? I'll bet you do,' he added with a quick smile.

'Yes, but…'

'Just write it down, Laura,' he said with a hint of exasperation. 'You never know.'

'Oh, very well,' she said, and did what he asked, writing the number he gave her down on the back of one of her business cards.

Then she bolted for the exit, thankfully not spotting anyone she knew on the way out. Laura was out of breath by the time she made it to the quay and onto the Manly ferry for the ride home, glad to subside into a seat in a private corner, glad to be alone with her still-whirling thoughts.

But, once her head settled and her heart stopped beating like a rock-band drummer, Laura knew she'd made the right decision, knocking back Ryan's offer. It was ridiculous to keep such a deception going, no matter how tempted she'd been.

What was that other saying, now? 'Oh what a tangled web we weave when first we practise to deceive'?

As she'd spelled out to Ryan, it would have been extremely difficult to carry off such a pretence without their dislike for each other shining through somehow. No, she'd done the right thing. The only thing. But she still winced at the thought of telling the family that she'd lied about finding Mr Right. She did have her pride.

No, she'd do what she originally said she'd do: make some excuse why Ryan couldn't join them this weekend. Then later on, if Gran continued to recover, she could say that they'd broken up because Ryan refused to get married. That would save her pride too. If Gran didn't recover—Laura's heart contracted fiercely at this thought—then it wouldn't matter. Gran would at least have died happy.

CHAPTER FIVE

BY THE time the ferry docked at the Manly wharf and Laura started off up the hill for the walk home, she'd become reconciled to her decision, except for one small regret. It would have been seriously satisfying to go home with a man like Ryan on her arm, she thought with a rather wistful sigh, just to see the looks on the faces of her aunt and uncle, both of whom never let an opportunity go by to point out what a loser she was in the dating department.

Of course the truth was that they didn't like her. Uncle Bill had resented her from the moment she'd been brought home to her grandparents' place to live and it had became obvious that his mother preferred her estranged daughter's daughter to the son he and Cynthia had produced.

Laura didn't think this should have been a surprise, since all the men in the Stone family were odious. Her grandfather especially. Jim Stone had been a male chauvinistic pig of the first order. His son and his grandson had taken after him, believing they were superior beings and that women were only put on this earth to pander to their needs. After actually living in her grandfather's house, Laura understood fully why her mother had run away from home as soon as she was old enough and why she'd married a man like her father who, though a strong man, had been compassionate and gentle in his dealings with people, especially women. He'd been a lawyer also; Laura had adored him.

She'd disliked her grandfather intensely and hadn't been at all sad when he had died. But even in death Jim Stone had been able to make her angry, leaving the family property to his son rather than his long-suffering wife. She'd tried to get her gran to contest the will but she wouldn't, saying that it didn't matter, that Bill promised to look after her until she died.

But that wasn't good enough, in Laura's opinion. The home which Gran had lovingly tended for over fifty years should have been hers until she died. Instead, she'd been relegated to the role of a poor relative, reliant on her son for charity. All her gran had been left was a miserable twenty-thousand dollars a year, not much more than the old-age pension. That was until Laura had had a little chat with her uncle and insisted that he bump the amount up to forty thousand at least, warning him that if he didn't then she would use every bit of her power and influence to get his mother to contest the will.

Naturally, her firm stance hadn't gone down too well, but he'd done what she had asked. Of course, he'd made it sound like it was all his idea. When Laura had seen how touched her grandmother had been—she probably wasn't used to the men in her life treating her nicely—she hadn't said a word. Several times, during the five years since her grandfather had died, Laura had tried to persuade her grandmother to come to Sydney to live with her, but to no avail. Her gran said she was a country girl and wouldn't be happy living in the city.

Yet I have a very nice home, Laura thought as she pushed open the gate which led up the path to the three-bedroomed cottage which had belonged to her parents and which had come to her when they were so tragically killed. Her grandfather had tried to sell it after she'd gone to live with him, but her darling grandmother—who had been sole executor of her daughter's will—had refused to give permission for the sale. So the contents had been stored and the house had been rented out until Laura had left school and moved back to Sydney to attend university, at which point she'd taken possession of it again.

She'd lived there ever since, mostly happily. Only once had the house been instrumental in bringing her unhappiness. But that hadn't really been the house's fault.

Laura inserted the key in the front door, knowing that as soon as she turned the lock and opened the door Rambo would come bolting down the hallway, meowing for food.

And there he was, right on cue. Putting her bag down on the hall table, she scooped him up into her arms and stroked his sleek brown fur. It was better to pick him up, she'd found, than to leave him down on the floor to trip her up.

'How was your day, sweetie?' she said as she made her way down to the kitchen.

His answer was some very contented purring.

Once in the kitchen she plopped Rambo down on the tiled floor and set about getting him his favourite 'fussy cat' food, steak mixed with chicken. She'd just filled his dish with the meat and shoved the plastic container in the garbage bin when her phone rang—not her mobile, her land line. Which meant it wasn't Alison or any of her work colleagues. The only people who used her land line were telemarketers and family.

Laura steeled herself as she swept up the receiver from where it was attached to the kitchen wall.

'Hello,' she said somewhat abruptly.

'I finally got you,' Aunt Cynthia replied with an air of frustration. 'I tried ringing earlier but you weren't home.'

Laura glanced up at the kitchen clock. It was only five-thirty. She was rarely home on a Friday night before six.

'You can always get me on my mobile,' Laura told her. 'I did give you the number.'

'Bill said I wasn't to ring people on their mobiles. He said it cost a fortune.'

Laura sighed. 'Not these days it doesn't, Aunt Cynthia. Anyway, what did you want me for? There's nothing wrong with Gran, is there?' she added with a sudden jab of worry.

'No, no, your grandmother's doing quite well, considering. I'm ringing because Shane asked me to.'

Shane was her vile only-son and heir who was a chip off the old Stone block. He'd tormented Laura from the day she'd gone to live with her grand-parents. His family had lived nearby in a smaller house on the same property. Thankfully, when she had finished primary school, Gran had sent Laura to boarding school in Sydney, a move which she'd appreciated. Her grandfather had objected at first on the grounds of the cost but her gran had stood firm again, saying the fees could easily be covered by Laura's inheritance. Both Laura's parents had had excellent insurance policies which had paid out double because they'd died in an accident.

Laura had quite enjoyed her school days—not her holidays so much, which her wretched cousin had made a right misery. Admittedly, he'd improved slightly with age, mainly because he'd married a modern girl who refused to put up with his boorish behaviour. In truth, the last time they'd met, Shane had surprised Laura by being reasonably civil to her. But Laura couldn't imagine why he would ask their mother to ring her.

'What does he want?' she asked warily.

'To find out if your new boyfriend is the same Ryan Armstrong who was a famous goalkeeper a few years back. His father told him that it was highly unlikely, given he was dating you, but I promised to ask you just the same. Because Shane said, if he was, he wants to meet him.'

'And if he wasn't?' Laura asked archly.

'What?'

Laura gritted her teeth. They really were a most annoying family!

'Yes,' she bit out. 'Ryan is, or was, a famous goalkeeper.' She only knew that because she'd been told of Ryan's international success by a sport-loving colleague of hers who'd been quite jealous about her securing Ryan as a client.

'Heavens to Betsy!' her aunt exclaimed. 'I can't believe it. Shane's going to be *so* excited. You know how much he loves watching the soccer.'

Actually no, Laura didn't know any such thing. She'd had as little to do with Shane as possible over the years.

'I must say I'm somewhat surprised,' her aunt rattled on, 'That you've got yourself a boyfriend at all, let alone a famous one.

'I was saying to Bill just the other week that it looked like you were going to end up an old maid. You're not a bad-looking girl, but you do have an unfortunate way about you. You state your opinions much too strongly. Men don't like that, you know. And the way you dress is…well, not very feminine. Still, I guess there's someone for everyone in this world. So how old is your Mr Armstrong? I dare say he's not all that young.'

Laura couldn't say a word for a moment, having been rendered speechless by her aunt's tactless commentary.

But, as she struggled to find her tongue, Laura knew that there was no way now that she was going up to that house tomorrow alone. No darned way!

'To tell you the truth, Aunt,' she said at last, 'I'm not sure exactly how old Ryan is. Middle to late thirties is my best guess.'

'You'd think you'd know your boyfriend's age,' her aunt said snippily. 'How long did you say you'd been going out with him?'

'We've been business acquaintances for two years. But we've only started dating recently.'

'Oh, I see. So he's not that serious about you yet.'

'He's *very* serious about me,' she heard herself saying. 'You don't think he'd agree to come home with me and meet Gran if he wasn't serious, do you?'

'What? Oh no, no, I suppose not. So what time do you think you might arrive?'

Laura closed her eyes and prayed that Ryan

would not change his mind and retract his offer when she rang him.

'Around noon?' she suggested.

'Could you make it later than that?' her aunt said. 'Say, around three? That way I won't have to do lunch tomorrow as well as dinner that night and lunch again the next day. That's a lot of work, you know.'

'But we weren't going to stay the night,' Laura protested.

'Don't be silly, of course you are. I've already bought the food and the wine. On top of that your grandmother is expecting you to stay for the weekend, not just for a few short hours. You wouldn't want to disappoint her, would you?'

'No, of course not,' Laura said, but her head was spinning. How on earth was she going to keep up such a ridiculous charade for that long? And what if Ryan refused to go with her? Giving her his phone number was no guarantee he would say yes a second time.

'We'll see you tomorrow around three, then?'

'All right,' Laura agreed somewhat weakly.

'And Laura…?'

'Yes?'

'Bring a dress to wear for dinner tomorrow night,

will you? I don't want to see you at the table wearing those ghastly jeans you seem to live in.'

Laura sucked in a deep breath through wildly flaring nostrils. She was about to launch into a counter-attack when she realised the line had already gone dead. She glared down at the receiver for several furious seconds before slamming it back on the hook.

If there was anyone who could get under her skin even more than her uncle, it was her aunt—stupid, self-important, insensitive woman! Laura felt sorry for her grandmother, having to live with two such impossible people. She deserved better after putting up with that wretched husband of hers for fifty-five years.

Thinking about her grandmother's feelings put some perspective back into Laura's growing frustrations over the weekend ahead. Okay, so she'd backed herself into a right royal corner now. Too bad. Gran was worth putting up with pretending to be Ryan Armstrong's girlfriend for longer than a few hours. And worth having to put her pride aside to ring him back and tell him that she'd changed her mind and wanted to accept his offer. If he prevaricated, she would beg him to come with her, if she had to. Hell, she'd even bribe him if she had to. Though what with, she had no idea.

The thought of offering him sex popped into her head out of the blue. It was such a crazy idea that she threw back her head and laughed out loud. As if the prospect of sex with her would persuade a man like Ryan to do anything! It would more likely make him run in the other direction.

Shaking her head, she marched back down the hallway to where she'd left her handbag, rifling through it to retrieve the business card she'd written his number down on.

Her stomach tightened into a knot as she picked up her mobile phone and punched in the numbers. For what *would* she do if he refused? What *could* she do? Laura felt sick just thinking about it. She hit the call button and started praying.

CHAPTER SIX

'RYAN Armstrong,' he answered quite promptly in his very male voice.

Laura straightened her spine and squared her shoulders at the same time. 'Ryan, it's Laura. Laura Ferrugia.'

'Laura!'

No doubting the surprise in his voice.

She could hear noise in the background, people laughing and talking, and live music playing. If she wasn't mistaken he was still at the Opera Bar.

Laura decided not to waffle; she wasn't a waffly person at the best of times. 'Is your offer still open?' she asked abruptly.

'Absolutely.'

'Thank God,' she couldn't help saying.

'That sounds somewhat ominous. What's happened to make you change your mind?'

'My aunt happened, that's what,' she said sharply.

'Sorry. Have I missed something?'

'I'll fill you in tomorrow during the drive up there.'

'Up where?'

'Didn't I tell you? Gran lives in the Hunter Valley. So does the rest of my family. I'm sure I told you.'

'You probably did. I remember you mentioning the John Hunter hospital.'

'Yes, well, the John Hunter hospital is not really near the Hunter Valley. I take it you're not familiar with the Newcastle area?'

'No. Never been up that way at all.'

'It's a relatively easy drive. You just take the freeway north and turn off at the signs to the vineyards. I usually make it in just over two hours. If I leave home out of peak hour, that is.'

'And where's home?'

'Manly. Do you have a nice car?'

'That's an odd question. Ah, yes, I get the drift. You want to impress.'

'You have no idea,' she said with so much feeling that he laughed.

'In that case, you'll be pleased to know I have a very nice car. A navy-blue BMW convertible. Will that do?'

'Wonderful. And Ryan, I hate to tell you this, but my aunt assumed that we'd be staying the night and I simply couldn't get out of it. Though you don't have to worry that we'd have to share a bedroom. Gran would never tolerate that in her home.'

But it wasn't her gran's home any more, came the sudden thought.

Surely her aunt wouldn't put them in the same bedroom?

Surely not?

But she just might…

Best not say anything, or Ryan might back out of the deal.

It was a worry all the same.

'So, what's your address?' he asked. 'And when do you want me to pick you up tomorrow?'

'What?'

'Laura, get with the programme.'

'Sorry,' she muttered and gave him the details he requested.

'What clothes should I take with me?' he asked. 'I'm getting the feeling that your family has money. Am I right?'

'They're well off but not seriously rich. Still, my aunt fancies herself a social hostess, so she'll pull out all the stops for dinner tomorrow night. But you won't need a dinner suit or anything like that.'

'What kind of place is it?'

'Years ago it used to be a large stud-farm for thoroughbred horses, with hundreds of acres of prime pastureland. But when there was a downturn in the horse-racing industry my grandfather sold off all the horses and went into cattle. Then when he died a few years back and my uncle took over he sold off most of the land to a property developer and invested the money, though he did keep a few cows. Nowadays, the property's just a small farm, really.'

'I've never been to a farm.'

'You haven't missed much.'

'I take it you're not a country girl at heart.'

'You take it correctly. There's something else I should tell you.'

'Shoot.'

'I have a male cousin named Shane who's apparently a mad soccer-fan and is sure to be at the family dinner tomorrow night. He twigged that you were once a famous goalkeeper and is dying to meet you. Are you all right with that?'

'Won't bother me a bit.'

'I didn't think it would but I thought you should know all the same.'

'That's very thoughtful of you, Laura.'

'You're the one who's being thoughtful. I'll be forever grateful for you doing this.'

'It's my pleasure. If you must know, I'm quite looking forward to it.'

'I don't know why. I'm terrified.'

'Yes, I can hear the tension in your voice. Look, don't make me wait till tomorrow to find out what your aunt said to force you to change your mind. You have to tell me now or I won't be able to sleep for imagining all sorts of crazy scenarios. It wasn't just because she found out about my goalkeeping past, was it?'

'No, nothing like that. It was what she said about me.'

'What did she say about you?'

Laura told him—every insulting detail of her conversation with her aunt, even the bit where she implied Ryan must have been ancient to be interested in her. She could feel her temper rising as she gave vent to her feelings of hurt and humiliation.

'Do you know she had the hide to tell me to wear a dress to dinner tomorrow night?'

'Shocking.'

'Are you making fun of me?'

'Not at all,' he denied. 'I think your aunt was very rude.' He paused, somehow managing to sound completely unconvincing, and Laura remembered his comment about her appearance.

She bristled. 'I'll have you know that I own several dresses. And quite a bit of make-up. I just don't choose to wear either to work. Or at weekends in the country.'

'But you will *this* weekend, if you're serious about impressing your family. It's not just me who'll be on show, sweetheart, but us as a couple.'

'You're not going to call me that, are you?'

'Call you what?'

'Sweetheart,' she bit out.

'Not if you don't like it.'

'I don't like it.'

'What would you like me to call you, then?'

'Laura.'

'Laura it is, then. And Laura...?'

'Yes?'

'Try to relax a bit before tomorrow, will you? You're way too uptight.'

'Sorry. I can't help it. I hate having to do this.'

'What? Pretend that you're in love with me?'

Laura winced. Did he have to be so baldly honest?

'I guess,' she said.

'You've been madly in love before, haven't you?'

'Yes,' she confessed reluctantly. Twice. First with Brad, and then with Mario. Finding out Brad was a selfish, greedy, amoral rat had been devastating enough. But it had been the super-charming Mario who had nearly destroyed her. Because she should have known better by then. Should have seen through his lies.

But she hadn't.

'Act with me the way you acted with him, then,' Ryan suggested.

'I could never act that way again,' she said coldly. 'It was pathetic.'

'That bad, huh? Okay, just don't freeze up if I put my arm around you or give you a little kiss occasionally. Strictly no tongues.'

'I should hope not!'

He laughed. 'I can see that tomorrow might be a stretch, but what the hell? We're doing this for your gran, right?'

Laura blinked. She'd almost forgotten about her. Ever since that horrid phone call from her aunt she'd been thinking more about herself and her pride.

'Yes,' she said, feeling ashamed of herself. 'Yes, of course.' There wasn't anything she wouldn't do for her gran. 'Ryan...?'

'Mmm?'

'You can call me sweetheart if you want to.'

He laughed. 'That's more like it. Now you just need to find a dress. Red would look good on you.'

'But I don't own a red dress.'

'Then go buy one! You have all tomorrow morning. And some sexy shoes as well. Have to go now, Laura, someone's trying to ring me. I'll see you at your place tomorrow at one o'clock sharp.'

Laura opened her mouth to protest, but he'd already hung up.

Dear God, what have I done?

But he was right, she supposed. Any girlfriend of Ryan's would dress sexily.

Laura hadn't dressed sexily since she'd split with Mario, which was quite a few years ago now. Frankly, she wouldn't even know where to start to find a sexy red dress.

But Alison would. Alison was right into fashion.

Laura pulled a face. If she asked Alison for help that would mean telling her what she was doing this weekend—and with whom. This would also mean confessing what she'd said to her gran when she'd been in the coma.

Alison would be hurt that she hadn't confided in her earlier. The two girls pretty well told each other everything, had done ever since their boarding-school days together. Confessing that she'd kept a secret from her would be hard but it had to be done.

Hopefully, she wouldn't judge her too harshly. Biting her bottom lip, she punched in Alison's number and walked slowly into her bedroom. There she sank down on the side of the bed and waited for her best friend to answer.

Please don't let her have gone out tonight, she prayed as the phone rang and rang.

A split second before it would have gone to her message bank, Alison's harried voice came down the line. 'This had better be important, Laura. You know how dreadful the children can be at this time of night.'

In truth, Laura could hear the sounds of arguing in the background. Alison had a boy of eight and a girl of six who didn't always get along, especially when they were tired. Clearly it wasn't the time for true confessions right at this moment.

'Sorry,' Laura said. 'But I am desperate. Could you get Peter to mind the children tomorrow morn-ing whilst you come shopping with me?'

'Shopping for what?'

'A dress. A sexy red dress.'

'Bloody hell, Laura, I almost dropped the phone just then. Did I hear you correctly? Did you say you wanted to buy a sexy red dress?'

'Yes,' Laura admitted, knowing that she'd just opened the floodgates to Alison's curiosity, which was second to none. 'Could I possibly explain tomorrow?'

'You can explain later tonight, madam, when I have time to call you back and listen to what I'm sure will be a fascinating story.'

'All right,' Laura said with a resigned sigh. 'Just be gentle with me. I'm feeling a bit fragile.'

'Rubbish! You don't do fragile. You kids, if you don't stop fighting I'm going to get off this phone and strangle you. Laura, I have to go kill the kids. I'll ring you back later.'

'Fine,' Laura said wearily and hung up.

CHAPTER SEVEN

'MY MIND'S still boggled by all this,' Alison said as she put down her coffee cup.

They were sitting in a café in Centre Point Tower, having spent a good two hours since the shops opened finding the right sexy red dress, not to mention a pair of equally sexy shoes.

'I mean, why Ryan Armstrong of all people?' she went on disbelievingly.

'You know why, Alison,' Laura replied patiently. 'He's exactly the type of man Gran would think was a good catch.'

'But you can't stand him.'

'I don't dislike him as much as I thought I did,' Laura admitted. How could she when he was doing this for her?

'Ah-*ha*!' Alison pounced. 'I get it. You've been secretly attracted to him all along. And he to you.'

'Please don't start that romantic rubbish, Alison.'

'But why else would he agree to this… This…?'

'Charade,' Laura finished for her. 'I told you—

he's doing it because he has a soft spot for grand-mothers.'

Alison rolled her eyes. 'Oh, phooey! He's prob-ably just doing it to get into your pants. Now that I've had time to think about it, I can see it's not romance he wants but sex. I keep forgetting not all men are sincere like my Peter. We both know what kind of guy Ryan Armstrong is, Laura. He's a player, with an obsession about winning. If what you've told me is true, you've been giving him the cold shoulder ever since you got him as a client. Am I right?'

'Yes.'

'Men like that don't expect women to give them the cold shoulder. They're used to being flattered and flirted with. You've become a challenge, Laura. You yourself said you were surprised at his asking you out for a drink.'

And to go sailing with him, Laura suddenly re-called.

'That was move number one,' Alison said wryly.

'But he has a girlfriend!' Laura protested.

'Who's away in Melbourne for the weekend. My my, how convenient.'

'It isn't like you to be so cynical, Alison. That's usually my bag.'

'Yes, well, I can see that you're in danger of being taken in by this creep. I mean, the guy asks you to buy a sexy red dress and you actually go and buy one. The Laura I know would never have done that.'

Laura sighed. 'I'm not being taken in by him. I just don't want to look like an old maid this week-end.'

'Well, you sure as hell won't look like an old maid in that red dress. And those beck-and-call-girl shoes you bought.'

'You told me to buy them.'

'That was before I worked out what the guy was really up to.'

'I hate to mention this, Alison, but it takes two to tango. And I have no intention of sleeping with Ryan Armstrong, even if he wanted me to.'

Which he didn't. But Laura could see where Alison was coming from. Her friend's view of Ryan's character had been tainted by what Laura had said about him in the past. If she met him, Alison would see that he wasn't some kind of sleazebag who couldn't go a weekend without sex. As much as it pained Laura to admit it, he'd shown her another side yesterday, one which had both surprised and impressed her.

'He's just being kind,' Laura stated firmly. 'Now, I have to get going. Ryan's picking me up at one. Thanks a bunch for coming with me, Alison. I would never have found that dress without you.'

'Don't thank me yet,' Alison said dryly. 'That is not any old dress. Even if he doesn't fancy you yet, he will when he sees you in it.'

Laura worried about Alison's last words all the way home on the ferry. It *was* a sexy dress. But not over-the-top sexy, she decided once she had the opportunity to have a second look at it in the privacy of her bedroom.

Of course the scarlet colour was a bit in your face. As was the wide, black patent-leather belt which was decorated with rows of silver studs. Still, the fashion world seemed to have become addicted to glamour and glitz during the last few years so it was hard to buy a cocktail dress which wasn't shiny or didn't have some bling on it. The same applied to shoes. The black patent high-heels Alison had talked her into buying had the same silver studs decorating the straps which ran up the front of her foot to the wide ankle strap.

Laura winced when she looked at the shoes again. Perhaps it would be wise to wear another pair of shoes, one which was less provocative, and decidedly less dominatrix-inspired. But when she rummaged through her wardrobe in search of something else Laura soon saw that there was absolutely nothing there that wouldn't look positively dreary. After her break-up with Mario, she'd thrown away all the sexy clothes and shoes that she'd happily worn for him, replacing them with a wardrobe which wouldn't have stirred a single hormone in any man.

Whilst Laura didn't actually want to stir Ryan Armstrong's hormones this weekend, she did want her family to think she was capable of doing so. If a by-product of this was that Ryan might look at her temporarily with different eyes, then so be it. She couldn't imagine that he would actually make a pass. Why would he when he already had a girlfriend who was no doubt providing him with plenty of sex? Whilst Ryan had a reputation for trading in his girlfriends with monotonous regularity, he did not have a reputation for two-timing. As perverse as it might seem, he was well thought of around Sydney as a man of integrity.

Up until yesterday, Laura had taken that opinion of her esteemed client with a grain of salt. But, now that she'd had more to do with him, she was beginning to feel that he could be trusted, which was a very odd thing for her to think about any man, let alone a swinging-bachelor type like Ryan.

Whatever, she didn't have time to worry about such matters right at that moment. It was getting on for twelve-thirty, leaving her only half an hour to finish getting ready then have a bite to eat before Ryan arrived. At least she was already dressed in decent clothes, even if they were just jeans and a simple white shirt. Overnight, she'd considered buying herself something else to wear for the drive up there—a skirt and sweater, perhaps. But it had taken all her time this morning to find the red dress. And, really, jeans were sensible for wearing on a country weekend.

Neither was she going to leave her hair down. She hated having it hang around her face all day; It was bad enough that she had to wear it down for dinner tonight. But she would compromise by putting it up into a ponytail which was a little more feminine than her usual style. Plus she would wear lipstick. Not red lipstick, however; the red-lipstick-wearing could wait until tonight.

Tonight…

Laura shuddered at the thought of *tonight*.

Then don't think about it, Laura, she lectured herself. *Thinking about it won't help. It will only*

*make you more nervous. The deed is done now
and there's no backing out.*

*Think of Gran if you have to think of anything.
Think of making her happy. Think of all those good
intentions you had when you first told her that
Ryan Armstrong was your Mr Right.*

Laura couldn't help it, she burst out laughing.
Ryan was so spot on. It really was rather funny,
his being cast as her Mr Right, because if anyone
was the perfect Mr Wrong for her it was him.

But her gran wouldn't know that, Laura conceded as she began to pack. She would only see
what she wanted to see, a handsome, successful,
charming, mature man.

What she didn't know wouldn't hurt her.

Hopefully.

Laura groaned. Somehow she couldn't get past
the niggly feeling that this weekend wasn't going
to go exactly as planned—that before this day was
out, it was going to be a colossal disaster!

CHAPTER EIGHT

RYAN glanced at the digital clock on the dash as he neared the street where Laura lived. Only a quarter to one; he was a little early. Not a good idea to be too early; he pulled over to the kerb to let a few minutes pass before proceeding.

Time ticked slowly by, during which his thoughts inevitably returned to what had happened when he'd rung Erica last night and told her his revised plans for this weekend.

Ryan shook his head at the memory of her reaction. Laura had been so right; maybe he didn't know women as well as he thought he did. Because Erica had not been happy. Not only that, she'd been decidedly jealous!

Being on the end of jealousy was something which brought out the worst in Ryan. When Erica started accusing him of also having fancied Laura and that this was just a ploy to sleep with her, Ryan had told her in no uncertain terms that if that was what she thought then it was time they went their separate ways. After which he had hung up.

The fact that Erica subsequently sent him several grovelling—then abusive—text messages over the next hour had only confirmed his opinion that he'd done the right thing in breaking up with her. But the episode had bothered him all the same. He'd turned his phone off in the end, but he suspected that more messages would be there if and when he turned it back on again. Though what she had left to say he had no idea. He'd already been called every derogatory name in the dictionary from a filthy louse to a 'something' libertine.

He hadn't been quite sure what a libertine was, so he'd looked it up and discovered that a libertine was a licentious and lascivious man who did as he pleased—which he thought was a bit harsh, though not entirely inaccurate. He did do as he pleased in the main. And it pleased him not to continue a relationship with a female who was hypocritical as well as foul-mouthed. It also pleased him to pretend to be Laura's Mr Right this weekend and make an old lady's last days happy.

The clock on the dash showed it was now twelve-fifty-three.

Time to arrive.

The house at the address Laura had given him came as a surprise. Not because it was grand, or large—it had possibly only three bedrooms. Federation cottages in good condition, however, were still worth a mint, especially when positioned high on a hill overlooking Manly Beach. He wondered if she owned it or was just renting.

It seemed an odd choice for a rental, he decided as he climbed out from behind the wheel and made his way through the front gate and up the flagged front path. The garden on either side was well tended, he noted, and the green paintwork around the front windows looked freshly done.

Not a rental, he concluded by the time he stepped up onto the ivy-covered front patio and rang the polished brass doorbell. Laura owned this lovely little house. He was sure of it.

Ryan was about to ring the bell again when the front door was swept open and Laura stood there, looking a darned sight better than she usually did. Gone was the funereal black suit; in its place were nicely fitted dark-blue jeans, black ankle-boots and a crisp white shirt with rolled-up sleeves and a turned-up collar. Her hair was swept back up into a ponytail and she'd put on some pink lipstick. All in all she looked five years younger than she had yesterday, and a good deal more fanciable.

Not that he fancied her. Not really; Erica was quite wrong about that. He would never have put himself in this position with a woman he seriously fancied. He was not that much of a fool.

'You're early,' she said, almost accusingly.

Some things, Ryan realised, could not be changed as easily as appearances. She should have been grateful, not irritated. He always liked it when people were on time.

Except at three on a Friday afternoon...

Now why did he have to think of that?

Ryan shrugged in an effort to rid himself of the annoying thought that something was eluding him here. 'Only five minutes. You're looking good,' he complimented her.

'Thank you. So do you,' she returned, if a little grudgingly.

'We aim to please,' he said with a smile.

She didn't smile back, though something flickered in her eyes. He wasn't sure what—more irritation, probably. Man, but he had his work cut out for him this weekend. It wasn't going to be easy pretending to be in love with Miss Prickly.

'I won't be long,' she said, whirling and walking

quickly back down the hallway. 'The bathroom's in there,' she said over her shoulder, indicating a door halfway up the hall on the right. 'That's if you want to go before we leave.'

'I'm fine,' he called back.

She was as quick as she said she would be, dragging a small black travel-case in one hand and carrying a plastic suit-cover in the other. Ryan stepped forward to take the bag, leaving her with the coat hanger.

'I presume that's a dress you've got in there,' he said as they made their way out onto the front porch.

'Yes,' came her brusque reply. 'Here. Hold it while I lock up.'

He was standing there, both hands full, when a cat suddenly curled around his right ankle, a sleek brown-coated feline who had 'show cat' written all over him. Until it peered up at Ryan.

'Good God!' he exclaimed in shock. 'Is this your cat?'

'What? Oh yes.'

'He's only got one eye!'

'Hmm, yes,' Laura agreed dryly. 'I had noticed that, Ryan.'

'What happened to him? Was he in a fight?'

'No. He had a run-in with a car about a year ago. Didn't you, sweetie?' she said, her voice turning soft as she scooped the cat up into her arms. 'Cost me a small fortune at the vet. Over three-thousand dollars.'

Ryan just stared at her. Over three-thousand dollars on a cat?

'Yes, I know,' she said, back to her droll tone. 'Not what you might have expected from hard-hearted Laura.'

'You're certainly proving to be more sentimental than I imagined.'

'Sorry to disappoint you.'

'I'm not at all disappointed. You should never apologise for having a softer side, Laura. It's what makes a woman a woman.'

'It's what makes fools of them,' she retorted sharply. 'Especially where men are concerned.'

'I can't see any man making a fool of you.'

'As I said last night, Ryan, you don't know women as well as you think you do. Which reminds me, what did your girlfriend say about your pretending to be my boyfriend for this weekend? Or didn't you tell her?'

Ryan realised straight away that the truth would complicate things unnecessarily. Far better Laura not know how badly Erica had reacted, or that they were no longer a couple.

'Of course I told her,' he lied. 'And she was fine with it.'

Laura shook her head. 'Amazing.' She bent down to drop the cat gently at her feet. 'Be a good boy, Rambo, and don't go on the road whilst I'm away.'

'He'll be fine being home alone?' Ryan asked as they made their way out to the car.

'It's only for one night. He has plenty of food and water and his own cat slap. I've asked one of the neighbours to keep an eye on him as well.'

'What breed is he?' Ryan asked as he laid the suit-cover down on the back seat then placed the bag alongside his in the boot.

'Abyssinian.'

'Ah. I thought he was a pedigree cat. Have you had him long?'

She shot him one of her impatient looks. 'What is this, twenty questions?'

Ryan decided to ignore her stroppiness. 'I'm just collecting some basic facts about you. After all, a genuine boyfriend would know about your cat, wouldn't he?'

Laura sighed. 'I suppose so. In that case, his name is Rambo and he's almost five. I bought him

after I...' She broke off abruptly, her mouth tightening.

'After you what?'

'After I broke up with Mario,' she went on at last,
her voice as bleak as her face.

'I see,' he said, wondering what exactly dear old
Mario had done to turn Laura into such a man-
hater. Had she caught him with another woman?
Or was it the classic deceit of his having been
a married man? His behaviour must have been
pretty bad to devastate Laura the way it obviously
had. Most women would have moved on by now.
Five years ago, she'd said. Wow. Did that mean
she'd gone without sex for the last five years? Ryan
couldn't imagine a life without regular sex. It was
as necessary to him as eating and drinking. Still,
he supposed women were different to men in that
regard. At least, some obviously were.

'Enough of the third degree for now,' he went
on, deciding to forget the awkward questions for a
while. 'So, what do you think of my car? Impressive enough for you?'

CHAPTER NINE

LAURA looked at the car and wished that she didn't find being in Ryan's company such a struggle. But from the moment she'd opened the door to him, she'd been thrown off-kilter.

She'd thought she was used to his good looks. After all, she'd seen him every Friday for two years and had never been rendered weak at the knees. But that was exactly how she'd felt a few minutes ago.

Perhaps it was the way he was dressed—all in black. Black jeans, black T-shirt and a black leather jacket. It was not the kind bikers wore but a softer, sleeker kind of jacket. It still gave him a distinctly macho edge. In it, he looked not just handsome but drop-dead gorgeous.

It had taken all of her composure not to stare. But she'd been rattled all the same, even more rattled when he had smiled and said how good *she* looked.

Thankfully, she hadn't done anything humiliating like blush. Unfortunately, however, she'd become defensive and uptight and, yes, downright bitchy. Which was the last thing she wanted to be with him today. If she was going to convince Gran and the rest of the family that Ryan was her real boyfriend, she'd have to stop being her usual sarcastic self and start being nice. Seriously nice.

To compliment his car would be a good idea, but she refused to gush. Gushing was going way too far.

'It's very nice,' she said. 'I like the dark-blue colour.'

'Get in,' he said, coming round to open the passenger door for her.

She did so, sighing with undeniable pleasure as she sank into the soft, cream leather seats.

'Comfy?' he asked.

'Very,' she said, and glanced up at him.

Bad idea. He was smiling at her again. God, but he was just so gorgeous when he smiled like that!

'You can't beat leather, can you?' he said, still smiling.

When her stomach actually fluttered, she gritted her teeth, put on her seat belt then turned her eyes straight ahead.

Unfortunately after he closed the door he strode

round the front of the car, right past her line of vision.

Even the way he walked was sexy, she realised, his legs moving with long, jaunty strides and his broad shoulders rocking slightly from side to side. It was a confident walk. Confident and cocky.

Laura sighed with relief when he moved out of view. But her relief only lasted until he opened the driver's door and slid in behind the wheel.

'I think under the circumstances,' he said as he gunned the engine, 'That we should put the top down.'

Instant panic sent her eyes jerking in his direction. She wanted to tell him not to do that, but already the roof was retracting and, really, what could she say? It wasn't as though it was a cold day. There was absolutely no wind and there wasn't a cloud in the clear, blue sky. There was no logical reason why she should be alarmed. But she was.

'You'll enjoy it,' he added, his eyes meeting hers. 'Trust me.'

Laura gave him a tight little smile. It wasn't him she didn't trust, she realised with a jab of dismay. It was herself.

Where had this sudden mad attraction come from?

Admittedly, Ryan was a very attractive man in a physical sense; as cynical as she was about the male sex, Laura wasn't blind. Okay, so he wasn't her usual type. Unlike her gran, she'd always gone for elegantly built males of average height who didn't tower over her. Big, broad-shouldered, macho men had always made her feel uncomfortable.

Ryan was certainly making her feel uncomfortable right at this moment, but in a disturbingly delicious and insidiously corrupting way. It was as well that he didn't fancy her, Laura realised. A blessing, too, that he had a girlfriend, otherwise she just might have been tempted to make a fool of herself this weekend.

Her stomach churned at the development of this highly unexpected situation. There she'd been, thinking she'd have trouble pretending to be Ryan's girlfriend. Now she was faced with having to control the urge to seduce the man!

Not that she would know how to seduce a man. She'd only had two lovers in her life, both of whom had done the seducing. She had absolutely no confidence in bedroom matters, and not a lot of interest these days, either.

Until this moment…

Perhaps her years of celibacy had finally caught up with her. It was the only reason Laura could find for the way she was feeling, so horribly aware of the man sitting next to her. Her sudden vulnerability to him brought a peculiar tension to her body which she could not remember experiencing before. Her shoulders stiffened, then pressed back hard against the seat, her hands twisting together in her lap.

'Relax, Laura,' he commanded as the car accelerated away from the kerb and hurtled off down the street. 'Everything's going to be fine.'

She wasn't so sure about that. Even if she got through this weekend with her pride intact she'd have to give Ryan up as a client. She could not bear the thought of going to his office every Friday afternoon with the same kind of feelings running through her that were running through her now.

It wasn't long, however, before she forgot about her pride and succumbed to the exhilarating and highly seductive experience of riding along in a convertible. Lord, but it was fun, whizzing through the city streets with the sun beating down on her face and the wind in her hair. It was impossible to remain uptight. Soon she relaxed back into the seat, thoroughly enjoying the envious looks on people's faces as they passed them by. Perhaps it was silly of her to feel pleasure at the misconception that Ryan was her boyfriend, but she couldn't seem to help it.

'See?' Ryan said after a few minutes. 'I told you you'd enjoy it. Want me to put some music on?'

'If you like,' she replied, having to work very hard to keep her voice cool and in no way flirtatious.

'Tell me what *you* like,' he countered. 'Music wise. I should know your taste in music, don't you think? And vice versa.'

Laura shrugged. 'I like just about anything which has a melody, a good beat and interesting words. I'm not into hard metal, or rap. I don't have a favourite artist or a band. I never was the sort of teenager who went ape over some singer. Unlike Alison who was—and is—simply crazy about Robbie Williams.'

'Who's Alison?'

'My best friend. We went to boarding-school together.'

'Ah. Perhaps we should leave the music off for now whilst you give me a quick update on your life so far. You don't have to tell me everything. Just the things you think I should know.'

'I'm certainly *not* going to tell you everything,' she retorted, thinking of Brad and Mario.

And she certainly didn't mention those two humiliating relationships. But she did tell Ryan about her mother running away from home to Sydney and eventually marrying her father, who'd been a runaway of another kind. Carmelo Ferrugia had been a lawyer, a refugee from Columbia whose first wife and children had been murdered by some very bad people. Carmelo had been twenty years older than her mother, a kind, compassionate man who'd spent the rest of his life helping people in difficulty.

She also told him about their tragic death in a small-plane crash when she'd been only eleven, about her years living up in the Hunter Valley with her grandparents and her time at a Sydney boarding-school.

'I always knew that I would stay in Sydney as soon as I finished school,' she added. 'And that I would become a lawyer, like my dad. I actually worked for legal aid for a while, like he did. But I didn't like it all that much. I found it a bit… boring.'

'So you moved on to Harvey, Michaels and Associates.'

'No, I joined another legal firm first, one which specialised in criminal defence.'

'You couldn't have found *that* boring.'

'No, I loved it. But I…um…'

'You what?'

Too late Laura realised where this conversation was heading.

She winced. She hated talking about Mario. Brad had hurt her, but Mario had cut very deep.

'I had a relationship with a client that ended badly,' she finally admitted.

'I see.'

'I doubt it.'

'No, I *do* see. I had a relationship with a client once. That ended badly too. It almost destroyed my business.'

Laura was shocked. 'What happened?'

'In a nutshell I had a brief fling with a client. When I broke up with her she did her very libellous best to bring my company—and me—to our knees. It was a close call, I can tell you. Makes you damned careful in future. I've never dated a client since. I dare say you feel the same way.'

'You could say that.'

'Just as well this isn't a real date, then. Still, I

don't think I have to worry about your ever getting obsessed with me, Laura.'

Oh, the irony of that remark, she thought as she turned droll eyes his way. 'I think you're reasonably safe.' *Provided you don't do anything stupid like make a pass at me.*

His laugh carried real amusement. 'You know, it's quite refreshing being in the company of a woman whom you can entirely trust.'

'Meaning?' she said a bit more tartly that she meant to.

'Meaning I would never have offered to pretend to be your boyfriend if I thought you liked me at all. Because let's face it, Laura, if that was the case this weekend could have complicated our working relationship.'

'I don't see how. Even if I liked you, you don't like me.'

'Not true, sweetheart. How could I possibly continue to dislike a woman who spent three-thousand dollars saving the life of her poor little puddy-tat?'

'Oh,' she said, and then did the unthinkable.
She blushed.

CHAPTER TEN

RYAN could not believe it when Laura's cheeks flushed a bright red. For a second or two, he was troubled by her reaction. But then he saw it for what it was: a natural response to the unexpected occurence of a man saying something genuinely nice about her.

Ryan suspected that Laura had been short of male compliments over the past few years, particularly with the way she dressed and acted. Clearly, she'd shut down after that disastrous affair she'd had with her client. He would have liked to know a few more details about that affair but knew better than to ask right now.

'I hope I haven't said anything out of order,' he said instead. 'There's no reason why I can't like you, is there?'

To give her credit, she regathered her composure with astonishing speed. 'Of course not,' she said with her usual brusqueness. 'You just took me by surprise, that's all. And, for what it's worth, I find

I can't continue to totally dislike a man who would give up his weekend to make my gran happy.'

He had to smile. 'Careful. We don't want to get too carried away with the mutual compliments, do we?'

'You don't want me to start lying to you, do you?' she countered tartly.

'Not till we get to our destination, at which point I think some judicious lying will be necessary, along with some judicious flattery and flirting.'

'Flirting!'

He almost chuckled at the horror on her face.

'Absolutely,' he said with a brilliant poker face. 'You do know how to flirt, don't you, Laura?'

'I've never been a flirter. *Or* a flatterer.'

No, he thought ruefully. You wouldn't have been.

'In that case, it's time you learned. Or are you planning on spending the rest of your life as an old maid?'

She shot him a mutinous look. 'How I spend the rest of my life is none of your business.'

'For pity's sake,' he snapped, feeling angry with her now. 'What is it with you? Okay, so some bastard hurt you way back when, obviously very badly. But he's only one man, not the whole male race. We're not all rotters. You have to move on, woman. Get back on the horse, so to speak.'

'Thank you very much!' she ground out sarcastically.

'You will, if you do what I say. Look, this weekend is a perfect opportunity for you to learn how to flirt. You can practise on me to your heart's content without having to put up with any awkward consequences.'

'No kidding.'

'You can cut the sarcasm for starters.'

Her sigh sounded...what—weary? Frustrated? Suddenly he saw that he was being way too forceful. It was a bad habit of his, trying to fix things and to control things. A result maybe of his childhood where everything had been out of his control.

'Sorry,' he said. 'I'm being obnoxious, aren't I?'

'Very,' she said.

'You can tell me to shut up, if you like.'

'Shut up, Ryan.'

He laughed. 'I promise not be so bossy when we get to your family's place.'

'Don't change too much,' she advised him dryly. 'Gran likes forceful men.'

'But you don't, Laura. I'm playing *your* Mr Right, not your gran's.'

'And you think you know what my Mr Right would be like?' she scoffed.

'I could hazard a guess.'

'Do tell.'

'He'd be a true gentleman, for starters. Slightly old-fashioned in a way. But there'd be no chauvinism in him. He'd treat you wonderfully, like a princess. He'd be passionate, but gentle at the same time. Gentle and protective.'

When he slanted a quick glance her way, he could see that he was right on the mark.

'What are you?' she asked with surprise in her voice. 'A mind reader?'

'No, but I'm a pretty good listener. I heard the way you described your father and I realised he was your ideal man. I dare say the man who hurt you so badly *seemed* like your ideal man, but it was only a façade. Underneath, he was anything but.'

Laura's grim silence touched an empathetic chord inside him. Ryan understood full well that talking about some things did not help. All it did was dredge up old memories which were better left unvisited.

'Sounds like he was a right bastard,' he continued. 'One best forgotten.'

Still, she didn't say a word.

'Time for some relaxing distraction, I think,' he said, and put on the radio.

'Now put your seat back a little and let some of that tension flow out of your body,' he ordered. 'And, before you tell me to shut up again, I think you should know that there's a small part of every woman who wants a man to be forceful with her when the time is right—which is now. So swallow that sarcastic remark which I'm sure your tongue is itching to deliver and just do what I'm telling you. Okay?'

He was pleased when she didn't object. In fact, she did exactly as he suggested—put her seat back, closed her eyes and let out a very long sigh. He wasn't quite sure what was going on inside her head, but soon she began to look a lot more relaxed. In fact, if he wasn't mistaken, she actually drifted off to sleep. It occurred to him that she might not have slept much the night before, worrying over the weekend ahead.

Still, it was as well that he knew the way north as far as the Hawkesbury river. Otherwise, he might have had to rouse her for directions. If he remembered rightly, the Hawkesbury was about a half-hour drive from where they were at the moment. That would give Laura enough time for a cat nap before he'd be forced to disturb her.

Five minutes later, he turned right onto the motorway where he accelerated up to a more enjoyable speed. The traffic thinned appreciably with the triple lanes and the powerful car ate up the miles. The suburban landscape quickly gave way to thick bushland on either side of the road which had been cut through the rocky hills. In considerably less than the half-hour he'd estimated, Ryan began the long incline which he recalled led down to the river and the small hamlet of Brooklyn.

He'd rented a houseboat there once, on a recommendation from a mate who said it was just the place for a romantic weekend getaway.

Ryan frowned as he struggled to remember the name of the girl he'd brought with him. Strange; that had only been about three years ago. Maybe not even that long. Yet he could not remember her name, or even her face. All that came to mind was his pleasure at being out in the open on the water. And the fact that he'd caught a fish.

He glanced over at Laura for a moment. This weekend would hardly qualify as a real romantic getaway. But Ryan rather suspected that he would never forget it, just as he would never forget Laura Ferrugia.

Ryan smiled wryly at this last thought. Impossible to forget the most irritating female he'd ever met!

CHAPTER ELEVEN

LAURA woke with a start, shocked to find that she'd been asleep for almost an hour and a half.

'Why didn't you wake me?' she demanded to know when she realised the time.

Ryan's shrug was nonchalant. 'I figured you needed the rest.'

'Where are we?' she said, suddenly aware that they'd left the motorway and were on a single-lane road. Panic set in until she realised they were on the right road, heading for Cessnock. 'I thought you said you didn't know the way!'

'I figured there would have to be signs. When I saw an exit which led to the vineyards, I took it.'

'You should still have woken me.'

'Will you stop fussing?' he said, his voice showing some impatience. 'We're not lost.'

'But we could have been,' she muttered.

'And if we had been? It wouldn't have been the end of the world, Laura. We both have mobile phones. We could have called and explained that we would be a little late.'

'Maybe, but I don't want to give Aunt Cynthia any reason to criticise me.'

'She won't criticise you with me by your side. She'll be putty in my hands in no time flat.'

Laura rolled her eyes. The arrogance of the man!

'Believe it or not,' he went on with a wry smile curling one corner of his mouth, 'I have a good track record with the opposite sex. Most women—especially the older ones—find me totally charming.'

Laura didn't doubt it. But no way could she let him get away with such self-praise without putting a small dent in his insufferable male ego, as well as reminding herself to be on her guard against him at the same time.

'Which is exactly why I chose you as my Mr Right, Ryan,' she said in droll tones. 'Because you have all those superficial qualities which pulls the wool over the eyes of most women. It's only the once-bitten, eyes-wide-open females like myself who recognise that charm like yours is just so much hogwash.'

He laughed a very dry laugh. 'And there I was, thinking you were starting to truly warm to me.'

'In your dreams, Ryan. Now concentrate on the road, please. We're coming into Cessnock. I'll direct you from here. It's a bit tricky getting through the town and out onto the right road.'

He took her directions without a hitch, and they were soon through the old mining town and turning onto the road which would take them to their destination.

'Not too fast along here,' she warned him as he whizzed along what probably looked to him a very straight, very good road. 'After all the rain we've had lately, there'll be a lot of potholes.'

Ryan slowed appreciably, which allowed him to take his eyes off the road occasionally to study the countryside.

'This is a very pretty area, Laura.'

It *was* pretty, she conceded, with lots of rolling hills and trees and well-looked-after properties, not all of which were vineyards. Tourism had spawned quite a few plush resorts to cater for holiday makers who enjoyed wine-tasting tours, plus five-star food and accommodation. It was also a popular place to retire to, with several new villages for the over-fifties who wanted to enjoy country living without the hassle of having to do too much work.

'I guess my view is jaundiced by my not being happy living here.'

'Just as your view of men is jaundiced by your not having been happy with one.'

Laura's teeth clenched down hard in her jaw.

'We all have jaundiced memories, Ryan,' she countered coolly. 'I dare say you have some of your own.'

How right you are, sweetheart, Ryan thought with a mixture of annoyance and admiration. She gave as good as she got. But shooting back poisoned darts must get exhausting. He couldn't wait until they got to her place and she would be forced to behave herself. Maybe even be sweet to him. The mind boggled at how she would handle it when he put his arms around her. Maybe even kissed her. Just for appearance's sake, of course. Even so, his heartbeat quickened at the thought.

'How far to go now?' he asked.

'Less than a kilometre. Take the next road on your right.'

It was a wider road, recently tarred and with no rough edges or potholes, which he commented on.

'There's been a lot of development along this road,' Laura explained. 'Several new wineries and a brand-new golf resort built on the land Uncle Bill sold them. We're just coming to that now on your right.'

'Wow!' Ryan exclaimed. 'That's some golf course.'

'It's not just a golf course, it's an estate as well. If you buy a house there you get automatic membership to the golf club. But it'll cost you at least a million. Crafty old Uncle Bill made sure a life membership to the club came with the land deal. He's crazy about golf. I suppose you are, too. Most sporty men are.'

'I wouldn't say I'm crazy about the game, but I like it well enough. To be honest, you have to be able to play golf when you're in the sport-management business. You've no idea how many deals I've negotiated on a golf course, especially at the nineteenth hole.'

Laura frowned over at him. 'I thought there were only eighteen holes?'

Ryan smiled. 'I see *you* don't play golf. The nineteenth hole is the golf club.'

'Oh, silly me. Slow down a bit; our driveway's coming up. There…' Laura pointed a finger to a spot just ahead. 'Between those two gum trees. You won't have to stop, the gates are always left open.'

'I can't see any house,' Ryan said, glancing around as he turned into the driveway.

'That's because you're not looking in the right place. That's it on top of that hill over there.'

His eyes followed the direction of her finger to what was a large two-storey homestead sitting majestically on the crest of a very distant hill. It was rectangular and colonial in style, with a high-pitched roof, and verandahs all the way around, top and bottom. Several chimneys more evidence of real fireplaces, no doubt with elegant hearths to go with the elegant architecture of the building.

'I thought you said your family wasn't seriously rich,' came his rueful remark.

'They're not,' Laura replied.

'Possibly you and I differ on what 'seriously rich' is.'

Unless this property was mortgaged to the hilt, then the owner, in Ryan's opinion, was seriously rich. The fences around the paddocks were in excellent condition and the cattle grazing on the pastures were fat and healthy looking. Despite his knowledge of country living being confined to watching the occasional programme on TV, Ryan could already see he was looking at money.

'I presume all the land leading up to the house

belongs to your grandmother?' he asked as they crunched over the gravelly surface.

'No. The whole property actually belongs to Uncle Bill. My grandfather—dear, sweet man that he was—left everything to his son rather than his wife.'

Ryan frowned. 'Why would he do that?'

When he glanced over at her, he saw Laura's face crinkle up in disgust.

'Because he was of the old school,' she said sourly. 'The one which believes that men should rule the world and own all the land.'

Mmm. Perhaps Laura's man-hating ways started long before that client she slept with. Still, Ryan could understand that a girl of Laura's intelligence would find it hard to accept her grandfather's chauvinistic—and decidedly unloving—ways.

'Was your grandmother very hurt at the time?' he asked.

'She was disappointed,' Laura said. 'But she didn't make a fuss, though she should have. I certainly did when Uncle Bill gave her a pitiful allowance out of all the money he'd inherited.'

'What did you do?'

'Threatened the bastard that I'd persuade Gran

to contest the will if he didn't give her a decent amount each year. Which he did do, grudgingly.'

'I'll bet you weren't too popular for a while.'

'I've never been popular with the men on this side of my family,' she replied.

Ryan laughed. 'I wonder why?'

'Why should I suck up to the opposite sex?' she asserted with her usual stroppiness. 'I'm as good as they are.'

'Yes, well, just remember that for the next couple of days you're playing the part of a woman in love.'

The expression on her face when he said this was worth all the money in China.

'I knew this was a terrible idea,' she muttered. 'I don't know what possessed me to do it.'

'Pride possessed you.'

'Yes, you're right,' she said with a deeply weary sigh. 'Good old pride—one of the seven deadly sins.'

She looked so dispirited all of a sudden that Ryan felt genuinely sorry for her.

'Not just pride, Laura,' he said gently. 'Kindness too. Let's not forget that. We're here to make your gran happy. What does it matter if you're forced out of your comfort zone for a couple of days? It's not like it will last for ever. Let me do most of the talking. You just smile and agree to everything I say. Which I know will be extremely difficult for you,' he added before she could say a single word. 'But it's all in a good cause.'

She was quiet for a long moment, but then she nodded. 'I'll do my best.'

'Good.'

Good!

Laura felt anything but good every time she looked at the man. She wanted to hit him for making her find him so darned attractive all of a sudden.

It wasn't pride that was possessing her at this moment. It was another of the seven deadly sins, one that terrified the life out of her.

Laura was not intimately acquainted with lust, had never been held in its thrall before. Both Brad and Mario had seduced her into their beds, and she'd gone out of the need to be loved, not the need to have sex with them.

But she wanted to have sex with Ryan. It was a most disturbing thought. Her sigh carried regret that she'd ever thought of this charade in the first place. Regret too that she'd given in to Ryan's suggestion and bought that sexy red dress.

Alison had spelled it out for her. That dress was

the sort which would get an octogenarian's hormones up and going. And Ryan was a lot younger
and hornier than that. It worried her, what might
happen if he did make a pass at her tonight?

'Come now, Laura,' Ryan said with a touch of
exasperation in his voice. 'Anyone would think
you were going to your execution.'

*An execution would be preferable to ending up
in bed with you*, Laura thought, keeping her eyes
firmly off his corrupting body and on the road
ahead. She tried thinking of what he'd just said,
about this all being in a good cause, but nothing
could unwind the knots of tension in her stomach. The niggling fear she'd had that this weekend
would end in disaster became steadily magnified
as they drew closer to the house. The sight of her
Aunt Cynthia standing on the verandah waiting
for them reminded her of that other fear she'd had
earlier today—the fear that they'd be put in the
same bedroom for the night!

CHAPTER TWELVE

ONE look at Aunt Cynthia gave Ryan a clue as to why Laura was so tense.

The woman was formidable looking to say the least, tall and solidly built, with a manner of the sergeant major about her as she stood there at the top of the front steps with her arms folded over her battleship bosom and her thick-ankled legs slightly apart. The skirt and top she was wearing was battleship grey as well. Possibly in her late fifties, she had very short, tightly curled blonde hair—probably permed and dyed—large facial features and the hint of a moustache above her thinly pressed lips. Her eyes were small and closely set, widening slightly as Ryan braked the convertible to a halt at the bottom on the front steps.

'Don't you dare get out of this car,' Ryan muttered under his breath as Laura automatically reached for the door handle.

When her eyes jerked round to his he bestowed

a one-thousand-kilowatt smile upon her, then bent over to graze her right cheek with his lips.

'Just do as I say,' he whispered at the same time. 'And smile, for pity's sake.'

She didn't smile, he noted. But she did as he said, staying put while he exited the car and strode round to open the door for her like a gentleman of the old school. Ryan deliberately didn't look up at Aunt Cynthia until Laura was standing up, her hand safely enclosed in his.

By then he was gratified to see true surprise on the woman's face, along with an almost welcoming smile. She'd even unfolded her arms by the time he dragged Laura up onto the verandah with him. Thankfully, the woman was staring at him and not at her rather robotic niece.

'You must be Aunt Cynthia,' he said, beaming broadly. 'What a lovely place you have here!'

When she stepped forward to extend her hand, her beady eyes, which turned out to be a faded blue, actually sparkled at him.

'We think so. It's so nice to meet you at last, Mr Armstrong.'

Ryan shook her hand with his right hand, at the same time keeping his left tightly clasped around

Laura's lest she bolt for it. Which she just might do, judging by the tension in her fingers.

'Call me Ryan, please,' he insisted warmly. 'And perhaps you'd allow me to call you Cynthia? After all, you're way too young to be *my* aunt.'

'Oh, go on with you,' she simpered in return, her cheeks going pink with pleasure as her free hand fluttered up to touch her hair.

Laura could not believe it—Aunt Cynthia, actually blushing. The man was a menace all right. But this was why she'd brought him with her today, wasn't it? To see this kind of reaction from her family, and Aunt Cynthia most of all. It was worth taking the risk of making a fool of herself with him in private to experience this moment of public satisfaction.

When her aunt turned stunned eyes towards her, Laura found a slightly smug smile along with a surge of confidence.

'He is gorgeous, isn't he?' she said.

Ryan was momentarily thrown, not only by Laura's compliment but by the smoky voice she used.

Wow, he thought. A guy could get used to her talking to him like that. Of course, he knew it was just an act, but a very convincing one. It looked like he didn't have to worry about her making a hash of their charade.

'Thank you, darling,' he said, giving her hand a little squeeze. 'You're so sweet.'

Laura almost laughed out loud at the look on her aunt's face. Dear, but it was priceless! Like she had something stuck in her throat.

'How's Gran doing?' Laura asked whilst her aunt was still floundering.

Cynthia blinked. 'What? Oh… Er, not too badly.'

'Can we go and see her straight away?'

'Perhaps we should take our things in first,' Ryan suggested. 'I'd like to freshen up as well.'

'Yes, yes, of course,' Cynthia said, quickly re-covering her composure to play the perfect hostess, gushing over the car whilst Ryan collected their luggage. He carried Laura's bag as well as his own, though he left Laura with the coat-hangered dress to carry, along with his dinner suit, which was also underneath a plastic cover. Ryan was glad now that he'd brought a suit with him, rather than more casual clothes. It wasn't a tux, just a dark grey, single-breasted number which looked good on him and fitted in with any occasion.

The house was as grand inside as out, Ryan noted, with a wide foyer covered in black-and-white tiles an elaborately carved hall-stand which had to be an antique, and an impressive curved staircase made of a rich red wood.

'It's cedar,' Cynthia informed Ryan proudly when he asked about it. 'There's quite a lot of cedar in this house,' she continued as she led the way upstairs. 'The house was built back in the thirties before the war almost ruined everyone, the racing industry as well. Did Laura tell you this was once one of the most successful racehorse studs in Australia? No, of course she didn't,' the woman rattled on before Ryan could reply. 'Laura's not all that interested in this place or its traditions.

'Now I didn't put you in your usual room, Laura,' she threw over her shoulder towards her niece who was trailing a little behind. 'It's way too small for two people. Shane and Lisa aren't staying the night, so I made up the main guestroom for you,' she said, opening a brass-handled door on their right with a flourish.

Ryan heard Laura make a small choking sound which, thank heavens, her aunt didn't seem to notice, perhaps because she was busy bragging about the people who'd once slept in the very large four-poster bed which dominated the room. She mentioned a past prime minister, as well as a governor general, a couple of English aristocrats and a Hollywood star along with her very wealthy lover.

'This house has a lot of history,' she finished up by saying.

'It's a very beautiful house,' Ryan complimented, having dropped both their bags by the door to wander across the room to the French doors which led out onto the verandah. 'And a very beautiful room.'

He turned to see a pale-faced Laura still standing in the doorway, staring over at the bed. 'But Gran won't like us staying in the same bedroom,' she suddenly blurted out.

Cynthia made a dismissive gesture with her hand. 'Jane doesn't need to know,' she said airily. 'She's not allowed to walk up the stairs any more.'

'So where's she sleeping?' Laura asked as she entered the room and draped the coathangers over the back of a chair.

'We've refurbished the old servants' quarters for her.'

'The servants' quarters!' Laura exclaimed, her face flushing.

'Before you blow a gasket, missy,' her aunt said sharply, 'Jane is very happy with the arrangements.

So don't you go making a fuss and making her unhappy.'

'Laura would never do or say anything to make her gran unhappy,' Ryan defended her, moving over to put a protective arm around Laura, warning her with a sharp squeeze not to lose her temper.

'Yes, I do appreciate that, Ryan,' Cynthia said through slightly pursed lips. 'But Laura has the bad habit of opening her mouth before her brain is in gear.'

'She *can* be a bit impulsive,' he said, tightening his arm again around her shoulders. 'But she always has people's best interests at heart. Especially her gran's.'

'I suppose so. But, as I said, Jane won't find out unless you tell her. Of course, if you'd *prefer* to have separate rooms, then...'

'Absolutely not!' Ryan broke in forcefully. 'I've been dying to get Laura away for a romantic weekend together. And, let's face it, that bed has romance written all over it.'

Laura might have enjoyed the flash of envy on her aunt's face if she hadn't been in a state of complete panic. Her worst fear had come about, that of having to share a bed with Ryan. It was bad enough having to stand where she was with his arm wrapped tightly around her shoulders, but at least they were dressed, and there was someone else in the room. How would she be able to cope lying side by side whilst wearing next to nothing with no one else in the room to stop... *To stop what, exactly?*

Laura knew full well that Ryan would never force himself on her. So what was she afraid of?

Herself again, of course. That self which even now was trembling inside at his touch.

'Now, my dears, I really must go downstairs and tell Jane you've arrived,' her aunt said brightly. 'I thought since it's such a nice day we could have afternoon tea together out on the back verandah. Could you join us there in, say, fifteen minutes?'

'No trouble,' Ryan said when Laura remained silent. 'See you shortly.'

The moment Cynthia closed the door after her, Laura twisted out of his hold. 'That woman is just so impossible!' she exclaimed heatedly. 'Fancy just presuming we'd want to share a room.'

'It's perfectly logical that we would,' Ryan said. 'It's not as though we're teenagers, Laura. We're an adult couple, having an adult relationship. Of course we'd be sleeping together.'

'But we aren't, damn it! And now we'll have

to—actually sleep together, that is. I mean, just look around you. There's nowhere else to sleep in here except on the floor.'

'Well you can count me out on that one,' Ryan said, marching over to lift his bag up and carry it over to the bed, where he dumped it down on top of the richly embroidered red-velvet quilt. 'I'm not sleeping on any wooden floor. Look, this is a very big bed. You can put some pillows down the middle if you like. That should stop me from accidentally brushing up against your very desirable female body and ravaging you on the spot. Which is exactly what you're thinking, isn't it? That I might not be able to control myself.'

Laura just stared at him for a long moment, before dropping her eyes and shaking her head irritably. 'That's not what I was thinking at all.'

'Really? What *were* you thinking, then? And don't say nothing. You are never thinking nothing, Laura.'

She turned and walked over to collect her own bag, wheeling it across the room before hoisting it up onto the bed on the opposite side to where he was.

Her eyes, when they finally lifted to meet his, were decidedly mutinous. 'I don't have to tell you what I'm thinking. And I don't have to sleep in the same bed as you. *I'll* sleep on the damned floor if I have to.'

Ryan scowled at her. She was one seriously irritating woman! 'Be my guest,' he said. 'Just try to do it quietly. I don't want to be kept awake with your moaning and groaning.'

'I don't ever moan and groan,' she snapped.

Ryan gave her a droll look. 'Now *that* I can believe.'

'Very funny,' she bit out.

'Actually, I'm not finding any of this at all funny,' he shot back. 'To be perfectly honest, I wish to God I'd never made this ridiculous offer in the first place. I must have had rocks in my head if I thought I could bring off pretending to be your Mr Right.'

The moment the words were out of his mouth, Ryan regretted them. Not that she didn't deserve some criticism—she wasn't making his job easy—but he hated seeing the crestfallen expression on her face. Hated having hurt her like that.

'I'm sorry,' he said straight away. 'That was uncalled for.'

'No no,' she said, shaking her head unhappily.

'You had every right to say what you did. The way I'm acting… It's silly and, well, it's just plain silly.'

'Then you won't be sleeping on the floor?'

'No,' she said, her chin lifting in an oddly defiant gesture as though it was a big deal, agreeing to share the bed with him.

'Good. Now I have a very important question to ask you before we go downstairs for afternoon tea.'

'What?' she replied, looking worried again.

'Where's the bathroom?'

CHAPTER THIRTEEN

LAURA showed him the door which led into an absolutely huge bathroom, the like of which would never have been seen in a modern house. There was a claw-footed bath sitting against the far wall of the black-and-white-tiled room, a brass-framed shower stall in a corner to its right, a toilet behind the door and a large marble-topped vanity table which had an equally large mirror on the wall above it.

'Wow!' Ryan said. 'I don't think I've seen a bathroom quite like this one before.'

'It is rather old-fashioned,' Laura said.

'Maybe, but I like it.'

'That other door there—' Laura pointed out before she left '—opens out onto the main hallway, so don't forget to throw the lock or you might have an unwanted visitor.' Though she couldn't imagine who. Uncle Bill and Aunt Cynthia would be the only others sleeping upstairs tonight, and the master bedroom was at the other end of the hallway, complete with its own private bathroom.

'Fine,' Ryan said and Laura left him to it, relieved when he closed the door and left her alone in the bedroom. It would be good to be away from his disturbing presence, even for a short while, give her the chance to calm the butterflies in her stomach and to find some much-needed composure.

Unpacking her bag, however, didn't help much, especially when confronted by the pink satin nightie she'd brought with her. Whilst not overly provocative, it was still rather low-cut, with spaghetti-thin straps. At least she'd had the foresight to pack the matching robe, though she could hardly wear that to bed, could she?

Her stomach contracted at the thought of how she would feel, sleeping next to Ryan tonight. She wouldn't be getting much sleep, that was for sure.

He emerged from the bathroom and she took the opportunity to escape.

'I won't be long,' she said, snatching up her toilet bag and dashing past him.

Ryan shook his head at her body language. He wondered what he could say or do to calm her down. It wasn't afternoon tea that she needed, he decided as he hung up his suit and unpacked the rest of his things, but a good, stiff drink. Either that or…

Ryan chuckled with dry amusement. It would be a bit difficult to relax Laura with some sex if just the thought of sharing a bed platonically with him horrified the life out of her. Which it obviously did.

The idea that she might not trust him to keep his hands off irked Ryan a little. What had he ever done to her? Okay, so he probably had a reputation around Sydney as a bit of womaniser. But he wasn't a sleazebag, or a cheat.

Not that making a pass at Laura would make him a cheat, given he and Erica had now split up. But that was beside the point. Even if he fancied Laura—which he didn't, not *really*—no way would he want to start something this weekend that could only cause him trouble in the future. Laura was a valued work colleague. She was also of a much more vulnerable nature than Ryan had realised.

To contemplate seducing her, even out of a perverse sort of compassion, went totally against his rules. Not that Laura would *let* him seduce her, he conceded ruefully. She would have to be attracted to him a little to do that, which she obviously wasn't, so why was he even having this stupid conversation with himself?

The bathroom door opened and she came out, looking a little less harried. Which was just as well, since he was beginning to run out of patience with her.

'Don't forget what I said about smiling,' Ryan advised brusquely as they made their way down the curving staircase ten minutes later. When she didn't say anything in reply, he stopped at the foot of the stairs to throw her a firm look.

'Come on, show me some of those nice white teeth you have.'

When Laura attempted a smile, Ryan scowled. 'Good God, is that the best you can do, woman?'

Laura winced. 'Sorry. I guess I'm nervous.'

'Lord knows why, with me by your side.'

'Are you always this incorrigibly egotistical?' she demanded to know.

Ryan shrugged. 'I suppose so. It comes with the territory of having been a successful goalkeeper. You have to have total confidence in your abilities or you're dead in the water, because you're alone out there. You can't let a single negative thought creep in or you're done and dusted. But you're not alone today, Laura. You have me to help you.

Though you still do need to help yourself. So, smile and make it convincing.'

She smiled, but she still didn't look like a woman in love.

'Only marginally better,' he said, feeling totally exasperated with her and with himself for being so affected by her. 'Here, give me your hand.'

When she hesitated, he suddenly grabbed both her hands then yanked her hard against him.

'The trouble with you, madam,' he ground out as he glared down into her shocked eyes, 'Is that you've been way too long between men. *And* kisses.'

He didn't mean to do it. Hell, he didn't mean to manhandle her in any way, shape or form. But all of a sudden his much-valued control slipped and his mouth came crashing down on hers.

For a split second, Laura froze. This was what she'd feared after all, Ryan making a pass at her at some stage. Not that you could call what he was doing a pass. It was more of an onslaught. He even dragged her hands behind her back and pressed them into the small of her back, forcing her breasts against the hard wall of his chest.

Laura knew at the back of her whirling mind that she could still escape his captive embrace if she chose to. All she had to do was lift her knee into his groin and he'd let her go, quick smart. But she didn't lift her knee or do anything else. Instead, she just stood there and let him do what he was doing. She didn't fight him. She didn't even make a sound.

But the moment he pried her lips apart and sent his tongue deep into her mouth she definitely did make a sound.

It was a moan, soft and throaty and full of sensual surrender.

Ryan moaned too, though not quite so softly. For a few more mad moments, the impassioned ravaging of her mouth continued before he abruptly wrenched his lips off hers, stepping back to stare down at her with shocked eyes. His prominent cheekbones had spots of red slashed across them, and his chest was rising and falling in a ragged rhythm.

Laura hated to think what *she* looked like, standing there with eyes wide and the back of a trembling hand lifting to hide her still-burning lips. 'Stunned' did not begin to describe her own feelings. How could she possibly have liked what he had done? Yet she had—more than liked, actually. She'd thrilled to his forcefulness. Even now the heat he'd evoked was still charging through her veins. She tried to feel ashamed of what she'd just allowed and enjoyed. Tried to feel angry with him. But she couldn't, and didn't. How utterly and perversely amazing!

Suddenly he smiled, a warm, tender smile which confused her even more.

'I don't think you dislike me as much as you think you do,' he said as he stepped forward to take her still-flushed face within the cradle of his large palms.

Before Laura could say a single word in her own defence, he was kissing her again, a much gentler kiss this time but still deep, his soft lips and less-savage tongue seducing her just as easily as the first time. Somehow her arms found themselves clamped around his waist as she rose up onto her toes, pressing herself harder against him.

'Oh!' a female voice exclaimed from somewhere near them.

'Don't move,' Ryan muttered into her startled mouth before she could spring back from him.

With considerable *savoir faire* he casually dropped his hands to her hips and turned her round. Laura tried to match his nonchalant attitude at being caught kissing, but she could still feel her face flaming. Fortunately, however, Aunt Cynthia seemed to be worrying about her own embarrassment, not her niece's.

'I'm so sorry,' she blurted out. 'I just came to see what was keeping you. I didn't mean to, er, um…'

'It's perfectly all right, Cynthia,' Ryan said smoothly. 'We're the ones who should be saying sorry for keeping you waiting.' And he gave Laura's right hip an affectionate little squeeze.

Laura didn't say a word; her throat was as dry as parchment and her thoughts in total disarray.

'I fully understand,' Cynthia said, gushing at him again. 'But Jane is very anxious to meet you, as you can imagine.'

'And I to meet her,' Ryan returned. 'Do please lead the way, and we'll be hot on your heels.'

During the short walk from the front entrance hall to the back verandah of the house—during which Ryan took her hand firmly in his—Laura struggled to get her composure back.

It was difficult; her head was all over the shop.

Seeing her gran, however, sitting there on the back verandah in a wheelchair, was enough to push aside any worry over what had just happened. Laura's heart contracted at how fragile she looked. Fragile and old.

'Hello, Gran,' she said softly, extracting her hand from Ryan's as she bent to kiss her grandmother on the cheek. 'How are you feeling?'

'Fine, love, just fine. Now that you're both safely here,' she added, glancing up at Ryan. 'So this is the young man you've been telling me about.'

Laura could not help feeling proud of Ryan as her grandmother's still-sharp grey eyes raked over him, no doubt taking in everything from his face, to his clothes, to his impressively built body.

'You've done well this time, granddaughter,' she said, smiling with obvious approval. 'How do you do, Mr Armstrong?' she added, and held out one very thin, wrinkly hand towards him.

He cupped it gently within both of his. 'I will do very well, ma'am, provided you call me Ryan and not Mr Armstrong.'

'Of course…Ryan,' she agreed, her smile turning a little coy. 'But only if you promise to call me Jane. Now, sit down here next to me and tell me all about yourself.'

Ryan laughed, but he sat as ordered. 'You must be planning on a long afternoon tea, Jane.'

'I'm planning on finding out if your character matches your good looks,' she shot back without missing a beat.

'Gran!' Laura exclaimed, slightly horrified at her grandmother's directness.

'It's all right, darling,' Ryan reassured her with a warm smile. 'I have nothing to hide. Besides, if I know you, you've already told your gran everything about me.'

'Well, yes, I suppose I have.'

'Then there's nothing to worry about, is there?'

Nothing except that you just kissed me twice and reduced me to mush both times!

Don't think about that, Laura, she lectured herself. *Think of the reason you did this in the first place. Think of making Gran happy, even if only for this weekend.*

It actually turned out to be rather interesting, listening to Ryan's answers to her grandmother's many questions. Laura soon realised that, whilst she knew about Ryan's sporting and business successes, she knew very little about his family background, except that at some stage he'd been brought up by his grandmother. It turned out he was the only child of a single mother, born and bred in the Western suburbs of Sydney. His father had done a bunk before he was born and his mother had died of breast cancer when she'd been only thirty-four, leaving him to be raised by his maternal grandmother who'd been a widow and lived on a pension.

'She had very little but what she had she gave to me,' he said with a slight catch in his voice. 'She was a wonderful woman. I loved her to death.'

'I presume she's passed on now?' her gran asked quietly.

'Many years ago, actually. Before I began to earn big money. She never saw me play for any of the famous European teams, though she did see my local team win a few grand finals when I was a teenager. Not that she actually *saw* them,' he said with a wry chuckle. 'She used to get so nervous that she would walk around the fields watching other games rather than mine. Then, whenever a loud cheer went up, she'd race back to see if it was my team scoring or the other one.'

'I used to get nervous watching Shane play soccer,' Cynthia piped up as she offered Ryan a plate of lamingtons. 'Shane's my son. Did Laura tell you that he's coming to dinner tonight just to see you? You're one of his soccer heroes.'

Ryan smiled as he took one of the cakes. 'She did mention it.'

'I hope you don't mind.'

'Not at all.'

And that was how the afternoon tea continued, with Ryan being charming in the extreme and Laura sitting there in the late-afternoon sunshine, basking in her grandmother's approval. She could not help looking at him all the time and thinking how incredibly handsome he was. Handsome and sexy.

Before long she started playing some crazy 'if only's in her head.

If only Ryan was her real Mr Right and not a pretend one.

If only his kisses from a while ago actually meant something to him.

If only he wasn't the kind of two-timing womaniser who was obviously not beyond taking advantage of the situation to try to get into her pants.

Alison had been right about that, Laura conceded with a twist in her heart.

But, even as this brutal truth hit home, she had difficulty ignoring the fact that she'd not only enjoyed his kisses, she wanted more. More kisses. More of everything a man like Ryan had to offer.

He would be a good lover; she could see that by his kisses. Wildly passionate, but tender and gentle as well. Brad had been an ignorant and selfish lover, uncaring of her pleasure. Mario hadn't been all that much better. Neither of them had ever kissed her the way Ryan had just kissed her, like he was a man dying of thirst in the desert and she was a sweet spring which would bring him back to life. At the same time, she had responded in a way *she* never had before—boldly. Brazenly. Blindly.

Laura knew that if they shared a bed tonight and he tried to seduce her she would be his for the taking. In every way.

This last thought truly shocked Laura. He already had a girlfriend, hadn't he?

But it didn't change a thing. This was why lust was one of the seven deadly sins, she realised—one of the strongest. One which called to the dark side which lurked in every person, which banished conscience in the selfish search for carnal pleasures.

Now, as she looked over at him, she started stripping him in her mind, seeing him naked and looming over her in bed tonight. He would be big down there, she fantasised. Big, powerful and forceful. She would cry out when he entered her, and moan when he began to move. Already she could feel him there, inside her, filling her totally, taking her to places that she'd never been before.

Laura had never had an orgasm during actual

intercourse before. But she would with Ryan; she just knew she would.

Such thinking took her breath away. What was happening to her here?

Thank God she didn't love him. Because, if she did, she would have been doomed.

Suddenly, she realised that her grandmother was talking to her.

'What was that, Gran?' she said as she lifted the tea cup to her lips and drained the rest of the stone-cold tea.

'I suggested you take Ryan for a walk around the property before it gets too late. It's lovely down by the creek at sunset and there should be a good one today.'

'All right,' Laura agreed. How could she possibly do anything else?

'Come and see me when you return,' her gran continued. 'I'd like to talk to you. Alone, if you don't mind, Ryan.'

'Not at all.'

'Bill will be home soon,' Cynthia said. 'He plays golf on the course next door every Saturday after-noon but he promised to come straight home after the game. Should be here by four-thirty—five at the latest, he said. You and he could have a game of billiards before dinner, Ryan. That is, if you play billiards?'

'I certainly do.'

Jane chuckled. 'I dare say you're good at it too.'

Ryan smiled. 'I'm good at most sports and games.'

Was sex a sport to him? Laura wondered ruefully. Or a game?

'Come on then, darling,' he went on as he stood up. 'Let's get going before the sun goes down.'

Suddenly, Laura didn't want to be alone with him. Certainly not down at the creek which was a very private spot, totally out of sight of everyone. She had little option, however, but to stand up and do exactly what had been suggested. To refuse would have seemed odd.

He took her hand, as she knew he would, and she didn't object, as she knew she wouldn't. No doubt they looked like lovers, strolling down the hill together, hand in hand. But love had nothing to do with the feelings which were zooming through Laura. She tried to say something, anything at all. But she remained silent. Ryan didn't say anything, either. When they reached the shelter of the trees which lined the creek, he let go of her hand and turned to face her.

'Tell me what you're thinking.'

She dragged in a deep breath which she exhaled slowly as she assembled her thoughts. No way could she tell him what she was *really* thinking. But she had to make some comment to excuse the way she'd responded to his kisses.

'I'm thinking you were right about my being too long between men. *And* kisses.'

He frowned. 'So you're saying that that's why you enjoyed my kissing you as much as you obviously did? Because you're sexually frustrated?'

She kept her eyes cool. 'It seems a logical explanation, don't you think?'

'True. But I can hardly make the same claim. I certainly haven't been five years without a woman. But I sure as hell enjoyed kissing you, Laura. Maybe Erica was right after all. And so were you.'

'About what?'

'You said I didn't know women as much as I thought I did. Erica actually went off her brain when I told her what I was doing this weekend. Accused me of fancying you.'

'Really?'

'Yep. I got so mad at her that I broke up with her on the spot.'

'You *did*?' Lord, but she shouldn't have been

quite so happy about that. But she was. Oh yes, she definitely was. How stupid could she get?

'Sure did,' he confirmed. 'I didn't want to say so earlier on because I thought it might cause you some worry. But she was right, wasn't she? I do fancy you.'

'*Really?*' Now she was even happier! Until she remembered that Ryan fancying a woman meant next to nothing. He'd obviously fancied Erica and look what happened to her.

'Yes, *really*. But my fancying you is not a good idea, Laura.'

'Why?' Oh Laura, Laura, did you have to sound so disappointed when you said that?

His eyes showed that she'd betrayed herself to a degree.

'You are a work colleague and I do not date work colleagues,' he stated.

'I see,' she said, not quite so happy now.

'You wouldn't want to date a man like me anyway,' he ground out. 'I'm not what you want. Or what you need.'

Laura shook her head from side to side. 'I'm not sure what I want or need any more.'

'Then let me remind you: you want a man who'll love you, marry you and give you children. That man will never be me, Laura. Because that's not what *I* want.'

Laura frowned at this last statement. What had happened to Ryan in the past that he never dared to risk getting emotionally involved with anyone? Something must have happened, because it wasn't natural to shun love. Everyone wanted to love and be loved.

'And why is that?' she couldn't resist asking. 'What have you got against love and marriage and children?'

'Absolutely nothing,' he bit out. 'It's just not for me. Look, it's as well that we've had this little talk. I would hate to think that I would do something tonight which we would both regret. Under the circumstances, I think you should ask Cynthia to put me in a separate bedroom when we get back.'

Laura sucked in air sharply. 'But I can't do that!'

'Why not?'

'Because I just can't!'

His eyes narrowed on her, with a glint of wicked humour. 'Is this your pride speaking, or something else? Don't tell me you've been secretly attracted to me all this time?'

'Don't be ridiculous!' she snapped. 'No one was

more surprised than I when I reacted the way I did when you kissed me.'

'I wouldn't say that,' Ryan said dryly. 'I was pretty surprised myself. Okay, so it's a matter of pride. In that case I won't ask for a separate room, but I think I will sleep on the floor. I don't trust myself to keep my hands off you if we share a bed. Hell on earth, woman, stop looking at me like that!'

'How am I looking at you?' she asked, trying to sound innocent but feeling anything but. She didn't want him to sleep on the floor. And she certainly didn't want him to keep his hands to himself.

'Don't try to play games with me, Laura. I'm way out of your league in the games department. Erica called me a libertine.'

'I don't believe you're a libertine at all,' she said, feeling angry with Erica for saying such a nasty thing. 'A libertine doesn't care about people's feelings. You obviously care about mine to warn me off you. A libertine would just take what he wanted without a second thought.'

'Would he now?'

For a split second, his eyes grew so cold that a shiver ran down Laura's spine. But then he whirled away from her and strode over to the edge of the creek. She stared after him, not knowing what to say or do. So she just stood there and waited. Eventually, the sun dipped down behind the hills and the air turned suddenly cool, at which point he turned and walked back towards her.

'Let's get back,' he said, and grabbed her hand once more.

But there was nothing warm or affectionate in his grip. She could feel anger in his fingers, but wasn't sure who he was more angry with, her or himself.

'I promise I won't look at you like that any more,' she said during their hurried walk up the hill.

'Good,' he snapped. 'And I promise I won't bloody well kiss you any more!'

CHAPTER FOURTEEN

'HE'S absolutely gorgeous, Laura,' was the first thing Gran said. 'I can't tell you how pleased I am for you.'

They were in the old servants' quarters, Jane propped up in bed and Laura sitting in an armchair not far from her. Cynthia had certainly done the room up nicely, Laura conceded privately, with everything Jane could wish for. The walls had been painted a rich cream colour. There was a brand-new flat-screen television sitting on a high chest-of-drawers opposite the foot of the bed and the old wooden floorboards had been freshly polished and varnished.

'He's a very special person,' Laura said, trying to ignore her disappointment over Ryan's decision not to take advantage of her obvious desire for him. It was perverse of her, she knew, but she almost wished that he *would*. She could not believe how much she wanted him to make love to her for real. It was cruel, the intensity of her yearning for him.

'I hope you don't think I'm being rude asking you this,' her gran said. 'But have you been to bed with him yet?'

Laura's hands tightened over the ends of the armrests.

For a moment, she wasn't sure what to say. But then decided to go with the truth.

'No, Gran,' she said. 'I haven't.'

'Wise girl,' her grandmother said. 'Playing hard to get is the way to land a man of the world like your Ryan. Though I doubt he's as tough as he looks.'

'What do you mean by that?'

'I suspect that underneath his macho façade your Ryan is quite a sensitive fellow. Reading between the lines, I wouldn't think his childhood was a bed of roses. It must have been hard on him, not having a father, then having his mother die when he was still just a child. Damaged children can sometimes find it hard to trust, and to expect happiness. In that regard you two have something in common.'

'I'm not damaged, Gran,' she said defensively.

'Aren't you, dear? I would have thought that any girl as attractive as you who reaches your age still single has to be somewhat damaged, for one reason or another.'

'Gran, that's old-fashioned thinking! Girls don't have to get married today to be happy.'

'That's tommy rot. Every girl wants commitment. And children. You do want children, don't you, Laura?'

'Of course I do, in due time. Now, Gran, please don't start dropping hints about marriage and children at dinner tonight. Men like Ryan like to run their own race. He'll get round to proposing when he's good and ready.'

'He's nearly forty, Laura. What's he been waiting for all these years?'

'For the right girl to come along, I suppose,' Laura said, but not very convincingly.

'He won't get a better girl than you.'

Laura's heart turned over at the compliment. Her gran had always loved her, no matter how she'd acted. Laura knew she'd been a difficult teenager after the shock and grief of her parents' tragic deaths. Not to mention having to live in a house where she wasn't exactly wanted. Without her gran's love she would have been even more wretched than she was. How on earth was she going to survive without her? Yet she would have to. And soon. There was a grey pallor to her grandmother's skin which frightened Laura.

A weary sigh escaped her grandmother's lips. 'I would dearly love to see you married before I go to meet my maker.'

'You will, Gran,' Laura said, blinking back tears. 'You will.'

'You'll have to be quick, my darling girl. I don't have much longer on this earth.'

'Nonsense. You'll live till you're a hundred!'

Her grandmother smiled a wry, knowing smile. 'I'll be content with eighty. Which gives you just over a month to get Mr Perfect to propose. Now, I think I should have a little nap before dinner, dear. I get very tired these days. You go make yourself beautiful for that man of yours—not that you don't already look beautiful. Being in love agrees with you.'

Laura tried not to look guilty. She longed to tell her gran that it wasn't love making her cheeks flush and her eyes sparkle but good old lust. Not that there was anything good about it. Or old, for that matter. This was an entirely new experience for Laura, which perhaps was why she didn't know how to handle it. If she'd been one of those girls who'd had loads of lovers she might not be so confused, or so lacking in confidence where sex was concerned. A more experienced woman would use sharing a bedroom tonight to seduce Ryan herself. She would not be letting him go all noble on her and sleep on the floor. She would vamp him into bed and enjoy his absolutely gorgeous male body all night long.

Would she dare do that? *Could* she?

Probably not. She wouldn't even know where to start.

Laura suppressed a sigh as she rose from the armchair and gave her grandmother a kiss on her papery-thin cheek. 'See you at dinner, Gran.'

'I hope you've got something pretty to wear,' Jane said.

It was then that Laura remembered the sexy red dress she'd bought. And the very sexy shoes.

Her heartbeat quickened at the thought that maybe she wouldn't have to do a single thing. Her outfit might do the seducing for her!

She beamed down at her grandmother. 'I have a smashing red dress,' she told her. 'Alison helped me pick it out this morning.'

'Ah… Dear Alison. She's been a wonderful friend to you over the years, hasn't she?'

'She certainly has.'

'She's a good girl. You're a good girl, too.'

Am I? Laura wondered as she closed the door.

Would a good girl want what she wanted? What had happened to her long-held belief that she would need to be in love before she could enjoy sex with a man? Why did she suddenly want nothing more from Ryan than his body?

Shaking her head, she began to make her way back along the hallway which would carry her to the front of the house, and the stairs.

The sound of muffled male laughter met her ears as she passed the door of the billiard room. Clearly, Uncle Bill was back and Ryan had followed Cynthia's suggestion that they have a game of billiards. They sounded like they were enjoying themselves. Laura could see that Ryan would get along well with Uncle Bill, who was a man's man. No doubt Ryan would know exactly how to act in her uncle's company. He was clever that way, she could see. He had more social skills than herself, no doubt a product of running his sports-management company. She often put her foot in her mouth, whereas Ryan seemed to know exactly what to say to please everyone.

Except her, she thought with sudden mutiny. He hadn't said what she wanted to hear down at the creek. Hadn't done what she'd wanted him to do, either. How dared he kiss her like that and then reject her?

Okay, so he probably thought he was being cruel to be kind, not sharing her bed tonight. Clearly, he thought she was way too vulnerable a female to cope with an affair with the likes of him. Added to that was his own wariness at sleeping with people he worked with. Both reasons did show Ryan as a man of surprising character but, damn it all, couldn't he see that he'd already gone too far? Nothing was ever going to be the same again anyway. She could not possibly show up at his office every Friday, feeling like this. So she might as well do her best to seduce him tonight and be damned with the consequences!

CHAPTER FIFTEEN

'LAURA! For God's sake!' Ryan exclaimed as he rapped sharply on the bathroom door. 'What's taking you so long in there?'

He'd returned to the bedroom around six-thirty to find Laura sitting cross-legged in the middle of the four-poster bed in the corner, talking to someone on the phone. Given she was giggling, he assumed it was her girlfriend, Alison something-or-other. Nothing annoyed Ryan more than the furtiveness of females when they talked to each other on the phone. If only women could be as straightforward as men, then the world would be an easier place to live in and life wouldn't get so damned complicated.

Laura did interrupt her conversation briefly to tell him to use the bathroom first to get ready for the dinner, so he had, all the while perversely peeved by her lack of attention to him. He should have been pleased that she'd stopped looking at him like he was her favourite dessert. And he should have been proud of himself for resisting the temptation to take advantage of the sexual frustration that she claimed she'd *have* to be suffering from to fancy him all of a sudden.

Instead, he'd gone about showering and shaving in quite a foul mood, even nicking himself once with his razor, which he hadn't done for years. He'd also forgotten to take his clothes in with him, forcing him to come out of the bathroom with nothing on but a towel wrapped around his hips. Now, Ryan knew he had a good body, but what had Laura done? Nothing; not a single stare in his direction. Instead, she'd nonchalantly gathered up her clothes and sashayed past him into the bathroom without giving his bare chest a second glance.

Ryan's considerable male ego had been severely dented, so much so that he almost decided then and there to abandon his resolve to keep his hands— and his mouth—well away from her. He spent ten gratifying minutes fantasising about what he was going to do when she emerged. First he would kiss her until she started moaning again. Then, when she had totally melted against him he would lift her up and carry her onto that incredibly sexy bed where he would show her that, even if she didn't truly fancy him yet, she sure would soon.

Unfortunately the passage of time had a way of ruining perfectly good fantasies, and at the same time of increasing one's level of frustration. Which was why, after Laura had been in that infernal bathroom for forty minutes, an extremely irritated Ryan started banging on the bathroom door.

'Cynthia said to be down in the front lounge at seven-thirty for pre-dinner drinks,' he said through gritted teeth.

'I'm having a bit of trouble with my hair,' she replied airily. 'Why don't you go down and make my apologies? I'll join you as soon as I can.'

'Fine,' Ryan bit out, thinking that maybe a drink or two would soothe his ill temper.

Laura sighed with relief when she heard the bedroom door open, then close. She wasn't really having trouble with her hair, or her make-up. She'd surprised herself by doing both very well indeed. The fact was she'd been ready for some minutes but just hadn't been able to find the courage to leave the bathroom and face Ryan, looking the way she did in her new dress and shoes.

Which was crazy. It was what she wanted, wasn't it—to see his eyes darken with desire for her? To drive him mad with how sexy she looked?

And she did. Oh yes, she very definitely did!

Alison had given her strict instructions over the phone as to how to present herself if she wanted to get laid that night: hair down and curled lightly around her face. Lots of dark eye-liner and mascara. The reddest of red lipsticks. And she wasn't even to consider putting some silly pin into the neckline of the dress to hide her cleavage.

Laura had gone along with everything she had suggested and the result was wicked! She could hardly believe it was her staring back. She could also hardly believe that Alison had been so eager to have her succeed in going to bed with a man like Ryan.

When Laura had first told her what had happened so far, Alison had been genuinely shocked—not by Ryan making a pass but by his backing off.

'I don't understand it!' Alison had exclaimed. 'Not if he's already got rid of the girlfriend. It just doesn't make sense.'

Laura explained that he had this life rule about not dating anyone he worked with. She didn't tell Alison about his near-disastrous fling with a client, as she felt that had been a confidential confession.

'But you don't want him to *date* you,' Alison had shot back, exasperation in her voice. 'You just want him to bonk you silly all night. Isn't that right?'

'Er…yes,' Laura had admitted, her throat drying at the thought.

'In that case, this is what you must do…' At which point Alison had relayed a long list of instructions as to how Laura was to look. And to act—especially after they returned to the bedroom at the end of the evening.

Laura had been laughing over her outrageous suggestion in that regard when Ryan had walked back into the room. Suddenly, she had realised it was one thing to talk about seduction techniques over the phone and quite another to go through with them; just having him in the same room made her hyperventilate with nerves. But she knew she would only have this one chance. So she'd hurriedly shunted him off into the bathroom, putting some calming distance between herself and the object of this insanely powerful desire. Then later, when he'd emerged—wearing no more than a towel, for pity's sake!—she'd kept her eyes rigidly averted from his breathtakingly beautiful male body and followed Alison's advice to act cool and indifferent to his charms.

'Your gran was right,' Alison had said earlier. 'Playing hard to get is the way to go. If I'm any judge at all of the male sex, then once he sees you in that dress and shoes you won't have to do much later on. But if he's still resistant you might have to go to plan B.'

'Plan B' was performing a none-too-subtle strip-tease.

Laura swallowed as she tried to imagine following that last piece of advice from her friend. She wasn't sure if she could be that bold. Hopefully, it wouldn't come to *that*.

Right now, she didn't even feel bold enough to go downstairs. Everyone was going to be shocked when they saw her, not just Ryan. They weren't used to seeing her dressed like this. She wasn't used to seeing *herself* dressed like this. It had been years since she'd shown her cleavage in public. Years since she'd spent the night in a man's arms. Years since she'd trembled at the thought.

Laura frowned as she accepted that she'd never felt quite like the way she felt at this moment. She might have become concerned if her brain had still fully been connected with her body. But logical thinking had become difficult since Ryan had kissed her earlier this afternoon. Her mind had shrunk to one focus and one focus only: to get him to make love to her tonight.

Now she frowned some more. For she didn't want

him to 'make love' to her, did she? That would suggest an emotional involvement with the man. Only a fool would fall for Ryan Armstrong, and she was no fool.

So, rephrase that, Laura Ferrugia. You want to have sex with him. That's all. Then, once this weekend is over, you don't want to see him ever again!

CHAPTER SIXTEEN

'GO AND see what's keeping that girl, Ryan,' Bill said when ten to eight came round and Laura still hadn't made an appearance downstairs.

Ryan had spent a sociable twenty minutes in the elegantly furnished living room, talking to Laura's cousin and his pretty blonde wife and sampling some of Bill's top-quality scotch. Laura's grandmother hadn't joined them for drinks but she would be at dinner, he'd been told. His earlier irritation had dissipated somewhat with Laura's absence. But it seemed his respite was at an end.

'She's probably still having trouble with her hair,' he said, repeating the excuse he'd made for her not accompanying him downstairs at seven thirty.

'Yes, well, Cynthia said dinner would be served precisely at eight,' Bill said ruefully. 'And when Cynthia says eight, she means eight.'

Ryan knew Laura wouldn't want to offend her aunt or anyone else in the family. This weekend was supposedly about impressing them.

'I'll go get her,' he said, and headed for the double doors which led out into the main hallway. He was just approaching the bottom of the staircase when Laura appeared at the top.

He couldn't help it—he stared. And then he swore, a crude four-letter word which echoed what he would have liked to do to her in no uncertain terms. Fortunately, he hadn't said it loud enough for her to hear.

'You'd better get yourself down here,' he managed between gritted teeth. 'The natives are getting restless.'

And so am I, by God, he thought agitatedly as he watched her sashay down the stairs.

No one would have recognised her as the drearily dressed creature that showed up at his office every Friday. He'd thought she looked pretty good today when he'd picked her up. But this was something else.

She was shockingly gorgeous in that low-cut red dress and those incredible shoes. He didn't know where to look at first, his eyes raking over her impressive cleavage before dropping to her shapely legs which were on show as she moved slowly down the stairs. He'd always thought her legs were good. But in those shoes, they looked unbelievable. Not wanting to ogle her like some lecher, he lifted his eyes back up to her face. No peace there, however. Made up, and with her expertly waved hair moving slinkily around her bare neck, she looked like one of the sultry screen-sirens of the forties and fifties. Ava Gardner, with a bit of Lauren Bacall thrown in.

There had been times in Ryan's life when he'd regretted things he'd done. He supposed everyone had regrets. But right at this moment he really regretted telling Laura that he'd sleep on the floor tonight.

'I think I made a mistake telling you to buy a red dress,' he bit out when she finally made it to the bottom of the stairs.

She seemed taken aback. 'You don't like it?'

He laughed a dry laugh. 'You know damned well that I like it. You look absolutely stunning.'

'Thank you,' Laura said, thrilling to his compliment. 'You look pretty good yourself.'

'In this old thing?' he returned, smiling a crooked smile.

It wasn't the first time Laura had seen him in a suit and tie. But usually his suit was business black, the shirt white and his tie a conventional grey or blue. Tonight he was wearing a single-breasted one-button charcoal-grey suit combined with a silk shirt in a burgundy colour and a striped tie in burgundy and silver. He looked every inch an irresistible man of the world.

She wondered momentarily just how many lovers he'd had. Hundreds, no doubt. Whereas she'd had the grand sum of two.

But she was going to crank up that number to three tonight, or die trying. Not of humiliation, she hoped.

Surely he would not reject her? She'd seen the hunger in his eyes just now. All she had to do was convince him that she wasn't the fragile emotional flower that he thought she was.

'Ryan,' she said abruptly when he stopped at the lounge and reached for the knob.

'What?' he returned a tad impatiently.

Laura cleared the lump which had suddenly filled her throat. 'I…er…don't want you to sleep on the floor tonight,' she blurted out, trying not to blush but failing miserably.

Ryan's eyes narrowed as they ran over her once more. 'I see,' he said, and she wondered what it was that he saw.

'So it was just an act up in the room just now?' he went on.

Laura winced. 'Yes,' she admitted, and blushed some more.

'There's no need to feel embarrassed. I'm flattered that you want me enough to bother playing games, since that's clearly not your style. Frankly, however, I'd much rather you were straightforward with me. I despise deception and hypocrisy and holier-than-thou attitudes towards sex. There's absolutely nothing wrong with wanting to get laid, Laura. As long as you don't make a big deal out of it.' He looked at her, banked heat in his eyes. 'Are you sure this is definitely something you want to do? Think about it over dinner and we'll speak later on. Okay?'

Clearly, he didn't expect an answer. Opening the door, he cupped her elbow and ushered her into the lounge.

Dinner was a triumph and a trial. Everyone thought she looked fantastic, and said so, even Aunt Cynthia. The food was surprisingly good, the wine superb and the conversation lively. If Laura didn't say all that much, no one seemed to notice. Once everyone had stopped complimenting her on her appearance, the attention had naturally swung to Ryan who was a much more interesting subject. Shane bombarded him with questions about his soccer career. So did Bill. Jane seemed content to just sit and smile at the happy couple across the table.

Laura could not have felt less content. Or less hungry—for food, that was.

She could not stop thinking about what Ryan had said. What if, because of her so-called sensitivity, he ultimately rejected her again? What if he did indeed sleep on the floor and leave her to lie in that big bed all alone, all night long? How could she bear it? She could hardly bear sitting here at this table, listening to everyone talking absolute rubbish and making each course last much longer than it should. Didn't they know that she wanted the meal over and done with in record time? She had to know one way or another what was going to happen. Not knowing was killing her.

By ten, dessert had finally been cleared away and they all moved back into the front lounge, where Cynthia served up coffee in ridiculously small gilt-rimmed cups that she no doubt thought elegant. Laura supposed they were. She didn't want coffee at first, until she remembered that coffee kept you awake. After that, she had her cup refilled three times from the large silver coffee-pot which they were told had once belonged to a French Count and which Cynthia had bought on-line. When Gran declared she was tired and wanted to go to bed, she asked Laura to take her. Naturally, she couldn't refuse. As she rose from the sofa, Bill also stood up, suggesting the men retire to the billiard room whilst the women cleared up. In the past, Laura would have made some cutting remark over this chauvinistic attitude, but decided to bite her tongue this time. She did, however, glance at Ryan, who smiled in wry approval at her silence.

'Thank you, darling,' Jane said when she was safely tucked up in bed. 'Now, don't let Ryan forget to take me for that ride in his car before you go tomorrow.'

Laura just stared at her grandmother. 'What ride?'

Her gran smiled a soft smile. 'You *were* away with the pixies at dinner tonight, weren't you, dear?'

'A little bit.'

'Thinking about that man you love, I dare say?'

'Yes,' Laura agreed. It was only a half-lie. Her mind had been full of Ryan but not with thoughts of love.

Jane sighed. 'I don't think you should wait for him to propose, dear.'

'What?'

'Before you go to bed with him.'

'Oh. Oh yes. I think you could be right about that.' If she waited for him to propose then she'd never go to bed with him!

'I am right. Now, off you go. It's time I went to sleep.' And she yawned.

Laura gave her grandmother a kiss and left the room, closing the door quietly behind her.

The old servants' quarters were just across the back hallway from the kitchen where she found Cynthia and Lisa busily washing up a huge stack of dishes. It still annoyed Laura that her uncle and his son felt that housework was entirely a woman's domain, but Cynthia didn't seem to mind. If truth be told, her aunt liked having total control in the house. Possibly, Lisa was of a similar ilk. Although younger, she must have been a bit like Cynthia for Shane to marry her.

'You know, Aunt Cynthia,' Laura said as she picked up a tea towel to help Lisa wipe up. 'You really should have a dishwasher installed.' It wasn't as though they couldn't afford it.

'What on earth for?' Cynthia retorted waspishly. 'They don't save you any time at all. You still have to scrape all the food off the plates, then rinse them down before you even load the infernal thing. Then you have to unload all the plates afterwards and put them away.'

'I suppose you're right,' Laura said, determined not to fight with the woman tonight. 'By the way, Aunt, that was a lovely meal tonight. Thank you for all the trouble you went to.'

Her aunt turned a surprised face her way. 'You know, Laura, meeting that marvellous man has done wonders for your attitude. Not only are you looking so much better, you've finally found some manners.'

Laura shook her head whilst Lisa grimaced behind her mother-in-law's back.

Laura was itching to say something seriously catty in return when Ryan suddenly came into the room.

'How's it going with you lovely ladies here?' he said brightly as he made his way across the floor of the truly large kitchen to where they were grouped by the sink. 'Need any help?'

'Heavens no,' Cynthia trilled, lifting her gloved hands from the sink as she turned towards her guest. 'This is women's work. Anyway, we're just about done here.'

'In that case, would you mind if I stole Laura

away?' he asked as he slid a warm arm around Laura's waist. 'Driving always makes me tired and I didn't want to go to bed alone.'

Laura was glad that she wasn't required to say anything. Talking might have been difficult at that moment.

'You go right ahead,' Cynthia said obligingly. 'We can finish up here. As I said, it's almost done anyway, isn't it, Lisa?'

'Absolutely,' Lisa concurred. 'It was lovely to meet you, Ryan. Shane and I have something else on tomorrow so we won't see you again this visit. But I'm sure we'll see you again soon,' she added with a knowing little look Laura's way.

'I'm sure you will,' Ryan said. '*Au revoir* for now, then. See you in the morning, Cynthia.' And he swept Laura away before Cynthia could land them with a specific time for breakfast—which she was likely to do. Cynthia liked to run the house like an army sergeant, with a time for everything.

But Cynthia's rigid schedules were the least of Laura's worries as she was steered with considerable speed along the hallway towards the staircase. Ryan's fingertips were digging into her right hip and his body language reeked of anger.

'What's wrong?' she blurted out when they reached the bottom of the staircase.

'Everything's wrong,' he bit out, and started pushing her up the stairs.

'But... But...' she stammered, totally confused by his suddenly aggressive attitude. He'd seemed so agreeable in the kitchen just now.

'No buts,' he broke in savagely. 'And no talking. I've had enough talking for one day. And enough thinking. I already know this is a bad idea. I know that neither of us might be happy about it in the morning. But I'm sure as hell going to be happy about it tonight. And so, by God, are you! Or you will, if you just shut up and let me do what I'm good at. Which sounds arrogant, I know, but there's no virtue in false modesty. I was a damned good goalkeeper and I'm a damned good lover.'

Relief that his bad mood didn't mean he still intended to sleep on the floor swept through Laura. At that moment, she didn't care if he was unbelievably arrogant—which he was. Though maybe he had good reason to be. She'd never doubted for one second that he'd be good at sex. And now she was about to find out.

A shiver ran down her spine, then right down to her toes, making her shudder all over.

Ryan immediately stopped at the top of the stairs and pulled her close. 'Don't go pretending that you're cold, madam. You're hot for me.'

He was right.

'I thought you said no talking,' she said huskily, and pressed herself against him.

Ryan laughed, but then he fell silent, his eyes turning to a midnight blue just before his mouth crushed down on hers.

It was a kiss which told a story, if either kisser or kissed could read between the lines. The story was one of total frustration, both sexual and intellectual. Neither could understand the attraction they felt for each other this weekend. It was a mystery to them both. But they'd reached the point of no return, where logic had no power and all that existed for them was desire.

When voices in the hallway below threatened to disturb the marvellous madness of the moment, Ryan scooped Laura up in his arms and carried her into the bedroom, kicking the door shut behind him. He didn't miss a beat as he charged across the room and fell with her into the middle of the four-poster bed. They kissed on and on, their limbs tangled, neither of them coming up for air.

Ryan was the first to lift his head and draw a decent breath.

'We're acting like horny teenagers,' he said with a ragged sigh. 'All speed and absolutely no finesse.'

With almost shocking abruptness, he rolled off her and right off the bed.

Laura could not help the groan of dismay which escaped her lips. Immediately, he sat back down on the bed, leaning over to cup her face with gentle hands.

'I didn't want to stop either,' he reassured her softly. 'But allow me to know what's best in this situation. I could be wrong, but I have the impression that sex for you hasn't exactly been of the bell-ringing variety in the past. If it were, you wouldn't have gone five years without it.'

Laura blinked, both at his intuitive conclusion and his rather amazing ability to take control of the wild passion which had been raging between them less than a few seconds earlier. She could not possibly have stopped, yet he had. Laura guessed that was what made him a man of the world and her a...what? A naïve fool? No, not a fool. Just much less experienced in sexual matters.

Perhaps not so inexperienced after tonight, she conceded with a rush of excitement.

'What do you want me to do?' she asked him breathlessly.

His smile carried a wicked edge. 'Now, that's a very leading question. Ask me again later. For now, I don't want you to do anything except just lie there and relax.'

'Relax?' He might as well have asked her to climb Mount Everest.

His smile turned a little wry. 'You're right, I don't really want you to relax. But I have something to attend to before proceeding.' And he stood up.

'What?'

'I'm going to light the fire. It's become quite cool in here.'

'I didn't notice.'

'You will, once you get naked.'

Naked...

Laura could not help shivering at the thought.

'After I'm done lighting this,' he said, moving over to hunch down in front of the fireplace, 'I want to undress you.' He glanced over his shoulder at her.

Laura swallowed. Her throat was horribly dry all of a sudden.

'Now, don't start thinking,' he growled before

returning his attention to the fire. 'It's too late for second thoughts. Or for worrying. You want me to make love to you and I want that too. We may regret it in the morning, but who knows? Maybe we won't. Maybe we'll look back on tonight and think of it as an incredible experience which neither of us would have missed for the world.

CHAPTER SEVENTEEN

WANTING a moment to recover herself, Laura got off the bed and went into the bathroom where she was momentarily startled by her reflection in the large mirror. She'd forgotten how different she looked tonight. For a split second it bothered her that Ryan's intense desire for her was nothing more than a superficial reaction to her suddenly sexier appearance. But then she shrugged the thought aside. Of course that was why he desired her. That was the nature of the male sex; their hormones were easily turned on by physical beauty. She had to confess that even the female sex could fall victim to such shallow attractions. If Ryan hadn't been so handsome, with a drop-dead-gorgeous body, she would hardly want to sleep with him tonight, would she?

By the time she emerged a couple of minutes later, the fire was crackling, with flames leaping high up the chimney. Ryan was back on his feet, leaning on the mantelpiece and staring down at the flames. His jacket and tie had been removed, and the top two buttons of his shirt undone. He looked pensive, and so sexy Laura could hardly breathe.

He turned and stared at her, his expression unreadable as his gaze moved slowly down and up her body. Gone was the overt hunger from his eyes, but they still called to the woman in her.

'Have I told you how incredibly beautiful you are tonight?' he said thickly. 'No, don't answer. And don't come any closer. I've changed my mind about undressing you. I want you to do it for me.'

Her eyes widened.

'Don't be shy. You must know you've nothing to be shy about. No, not the shoes; leave the shoes on. The belt first. Then the dress—but not over your head. Undo the zip then slide it off your shoulders.'

She did as he asked, her hands shaking, her heart thudding so fast and so loudly behind her ribs she thought it must surely go into cardiac arrest. By the time she reached to push the dress off her shoulders, her whole body was trembling. The thought of standing there before him in nothing but a black satin thong and a pair of high heels was both daunting and horribly exciting. As her fingers curled over the edge of the neckline, her nipples tightened further, as did her belly.

And then it was done, the red silk dress pooling at her feet with a soft whooshing sound. Her spine and shoulders straightened as he stared at her, and for a long moment neither of them moved or spoke.

But then he sighed. 'I'm not sure one night is going to be enough,' he muttered in gravelly tones.

She should not have been thrilled by his words, but she was.

'Come here,' he commanded.

Where did she find the courage to walk almost naked towards him?

Possibly courage wasn't an issue when she was so turned on that nothing mattered any more except that his eyes stay fixed on her bared breasts.

Which they did.

'Stop,' he commanded again when she was within arm's reach of him.

She stopped, her heartbeat momentarily suspended as she waited for him to reach out and touch her. When he did—brushing the back of one hand across her stunningly erect nipples—a lightning rod of electricity zapped through her body, making her gasp.

'Turn around,' was his next surprising order.

She teetered a little on her high heels as she did so.

'Steady,' he directed, taking a firm hold of her

shoulders from behind. 'Now, move your legs apart a little.'

Such a small, insignificant movement but, oh, what incredible feelings it evoked. She'd never felt so wicked. Or so wanton.

Her head literally spun. Was this the kind of thing he did with all his women? Stripped them, not just of their clothes but their conscience and their pride? No, no, that last bit wasn't right; her pride wasn't at risk here. She didn't feel in any way humiliated by the things he'd asked her to do. She'd seen the admiration flare in his eyes when he'd looked over her near-naked body. Laura had felt perversely proud of herself at that moment, perhaps because she knew he'd looked upon more beautiful bodies than hers. Yet he still seemed to find her very desirable.

I'm not sure one night is going to be enough, he'd said.

Not enough for her either, she suspected, if this was his idea of foreplay. What next? she wondered as an erotic tremor trickled down her spine to where her tightly held buttocks were quivering with anticipation.

He suddenly pressed himself up against her back, his left hand dropping from her shoulder to take possession of her left breast, whilst his right hand slid across to push her hair back from her face and neck. Her head tipped sideways when he put his mouth so close to her ear that his hot breath made her shudder.

'I think,' he murmured, 'That it's time to go to bed now. What do you think, beautiful?'

'I can't think at all,' she returned shakily. And wasn't *that* the truth!

'God, but I love seeing you like this,' he ground out, cupping her chin and twisting her head far enough around so that their eyes could meet.

'Like what?'

'All hot and bothered.' His eyes glittered down at her whilst he moved his outstretched palm back and forth across her by-then exquisitely sensitised nipple.

A tortured moan escaped her parted lips. 'You *are* a libertine,' she accused breathlessly.

'Not quite,' he retorted. 'But I could easily become one tonight.'

Ryan struggled for control as he scooped her up and carried her over to the bed. He struggled to calm his flesh, which was clammering wildly for a quick release. Not just quick—savage. He wanted to throw her onto that bed, rip off her panties and just ram himself into her.

Rough sex, however, was not something Ryan ever entertained. He prided himself on being an imaginative lover, but always a tender one. He never indulged in anything which smacked of violence. The thought of making a woman cry out with pain was anathema to him.

Okay, so some women liked it rough, he reminded himself as he laid her down across the bed. But he couldn't imagine that Laura would be one of them. Clearly she had believed, up until this life-changing moment, that she needed to be in love to enjoy sex. Which was a fallacy, of course. Sex was a basic human function much the same as eating and sleeping; you didn't need to be in love to enjoy either of those. Ryan had never been in love in his life and he sure as hell enjoyed all three.

Despite knowing deep down that he was making a big mistake taking a work colleague to bed— *business and pleasure don't mix, remember?*— Ryan told himself that he might actually do Laura a good turn by proving that sex and love didn't have to be joined at the hip. After all, it wasn't healthy for her to continue living without a man in her life. Her responses tonight had already shown him that she wasn't the ice queen she'd been pretending to be with him these past two years. Far from it.

By the time he sat down beside her on the bed and reached for her left foot, Ryan had almost convinced himself that what he was about to do had a noble side to it.

Almost...

Laura clenched her teeth hard in her jaw as Ryan slowly undid the ankle strap on her shoe then eased it off her foot. Where did he learn to touch a woman like that so softly and so gently? She would have thought a goalkeeper's hands would be harder and rougher. But, no, they had the sensitivity and the skill of a surgeon. Every time one of his fingertips touched her flesh, an electric current ran up her legs.

'I've always admired your dainty feet with their slender ankles,' he said as he dropped the shoe onto the bedside rug and moved onto her other foot. 'And, whilst I adore these particular shoes, I can't risk leaving them on right now. The thought of your digging their lethal-looking heels into my back does not appeal.'

When an image popped into Laura's head of exactly how she might manage to dig her heels into Ryan's back, her heartbeat went from a fast trot to a wild gallop, her mouth falling open as she sucked in some much-needed air. But when the second shoe was dispensed with and his hands started travelling up her legs she found herself holding her breath once again. By the time he made it to the tops of her thighs, she had to breathe or die.

Her gasp brought his eyes to her flushed face.

'These have to go as well, Laura,' he told her, hooking his fingers under the sides of her panties and peeling them down her legs, all the while holding her eyes.

At last, he looked at her there.

By then Laura found it impossible to speak.

She was dying for him to touch her more intimately, but dreading it too. She knew she would be wet down there. She could feel it.

'Ryan,' she managed to blurt out when his finger moved perilously close.

Too late. He was there, and it felt incredible.

Her moan brought his eyes back to hers.

'You have a problem?' he asked, but without stopping. He was still using just the one finger, but it knew exactly where to go and what to touch, an erotic weapon of total seduction.

Her face twisted into a grimace which reflected her dilemma. She was going to come. And, whilst she was dying for release, it was not what she wanted. She wanted to come with him inside her.

'I...I... You have to stop!' she cried out.

He stopped. Just in time.

Laura shuddered with relief.

His head cocked to one side as he frowned down at her. 'Would you like to tell me why I had to stop? It wasn't because you weren't liking what I was doing. I could tell.'

She gnawed at her bottom lip and looked away.

'I won't know what you want if you don't tell me,' he said softly, and quite sensibly.

So she told him, her voice faltering and her face flaming with embarrassment.

'Is that all?' he said, sounding and looking pleased. 'Just give me a minute or two.'

He stripped off with considerable speed, chucking his clothes onto a nearby chair and not stopping until he was down to his underpants. At that point he did hesitate, first to go over to put another log on the fire then to search through his jacket pockets for his wallet, out of which he extracted two foil packets.

Laura could not believe that she hadn't thought of

protection herself. Just as well Ryan wasn't so silly. But then he wouldn't be, would he? she thought ruefully. Not a man of his extensive experience!

Laura did her best to put her sensible head back on, but it was all to no avail when Ryan stepped out of his underpants. Oh dear, oh dear; she'd known he would be built like that. He was seriously impressive. His body was the sort of body that you saw on billboards advertising jeans or male Y-fronts. He could easily have made it as a male model. And he was all hers—for tonight, anyway.

This last thought brought excitement, but apprehension as well. Despite knowing she was way beyond changing her mind at this critical stage, Laura could not dismiss the niggling feeling that going to bed with Ryan would change her life in ways which might not be all good. She might have given the consequences of tonight's impulsive actions some more thought if a naked Ryan hadn't joined her on the bed at that point.

'Only got two of these, I'm afraid,' he said as he placed the condoms next to the lamp on the bedside chest. 'But they'll be enough. For now...'

When he pulled her round and rolled on top of her, Laura gasped at the weight of his body. But, as soon as he propped his upper body up on his elbows on either side of her chest, the feeling of pressure lightened considerably.

'Open your legs wide, Laura,' he commanded, 'And lift your knees up. Yes, that's the way, sweetheart. This could take a few seconds.'

Without using his hands in any way, he angled himself at her entrance but he didn't push himself in. Instead, he rocked back and forth and rubbed himself against her until she was almost at screaming point. She could feel her whole insides squeezing tighter and tighter, desperate to feel his flesh filling hers.

'Oh please,' she heard herself beg at last. 'Please…'

Only then did he enter her. But still not very far.

'Lift your feet and wrap them high around my waist,' he ordered her. 'That's it. Now rock back and forth with your hips. Hell, yes, that's the way.'

Laura followed his instructions until he was buried in her to the hilt, his flesh filling hers like a sword in its scabbard. Only then did he start to move, repeatedly pulling back a few inches before surging forward until he could go no further. Each thrust brought a gasp of pleasure from her lips, along with an increase in the most maddening frustration. As her body twisted tighter and tighter with sexual tension, her nails began clawing at his back, her heels digging into his buttocks. He responded by thrusting into her even more powerfully, and suddenly she came, her head thrashing from side to side as her flesh convulsed wildly around his. She'd never experienced anything like it before in her life. It was incredible!

'Yes, *yes*!' she cried.

And it was whilst her head was still whirling with the wonder of it all that Ryan came too, his whole body shuddering as it found release. He cried out as well, a loud, raw sound which reminded her of a creature from the jungle— Tarzan, maybe. Or possibly something less human.

So this was sex at its most primal level, Laura realised dazedly as she clung to his shuddering body. The kind animals indulged in. She could not pretend there were any fine emotions involved in their mating. They weren't in love. They barely liked each other.

No, that wasn't true any more. Not for her, anyway. She did like Ryan in a perverse kind of way. But she wasn't in love with him, despite having given him her body.

This last realisation came as a great relief. Maybe she would survive having a strictly sexual fling

with him after all. Maybe she wouldn't do anything so foolish as to fall for him. She'd already
fallen for two Mr Wrongs in her life. A third could
prove fatal, if not to her sanity then at least to her
soul. Because falling for *her* would never be on
Ryan's agenda. He'd spelled it out for her already
in no uncertain terms. He didn't do love, or marriage, or long-term commitment. Sex for him was
just a physical pleasure, to be indulged in regularly,
the same way he regularly ate and slept. Okay, so
he did stick to only one bed partner at a time, but
he always moved on. *Always.* She should never
forget that.

Finally, his head lifted from where it had dropped
down on the bed just above her left shoulder.

'Amazing,' he said with an almost surprised look
on his face. 'Was that as good for you as it was for
me?'

What could she say? It was way too late to be
coy with him.

'It was wonderful,' she said truthfully.

He smiled. 'Tired?'

She shook her head.

'Great,' he said, and after giving her a brief peck
on the lips he abruptly withdrew, his reverse action
forcing her legs to unwrap from around his waist

and drop back down onto the bed. 'Have to go to the bathroom,' he said. 'Don't go away, now.'

Laura could not help it—she laughed. Wild horses wouldn't have been able to drag her out of this bed. But as she lay there, waiting for Ryan to return, her infernal female mind did start worrying about how she might feel in the morning. Not ashamed, she decided with a surge of defiance; she wasn't doing anything to be ashamed of. Ryan had broken up with Erica, after all. There was nothing to be ashamed of in consenting sex between two free adults.

Nevertheless, she found herself reaching for some bedclothes so that she wouldn't be lying there spreadeagled and stark naked when he returned. Which was really quite hypocritical of her, Laura realised after she pulled the sheet up over her breasts. Because, in truth, she'd rather liked being naked in front of him. Had liked seeing the admiration in his eyes. But she kept the sheet up all the same. Maybe she needed him with her to be bold.

The sound of water running strongly in the bathroom soon brought a frown. Maybe he intended to have another shower. Hopefully, it would be a quick one. She didn't trust herself not to start regretting what she was doing if she was left alone for too long.

Unfortunately, time ticked away and still the taps ran.

So did her worrying thoughts. It actually wasn't how she would feel tomorrow morning that bothered her, Laura finally accepted, but the future in general. What would she do if Ryan wanted to extend their affair beyond this weekend? Hadn't he said that one night might not be enough? And, whilst she'd been both thrilled and flattered by his words, she wasn't sure that to keep sleeping with him would be wise. She might not be in love with him at this stage, but how long would it be before her emotions did become involved? She really wasn't one of those women who would be content with nothing more from a man but his body.

At least, so she thought, until the running water suddenly stopped, the bathroom door was yanked open and that absolutely gorgeous male body walked back into the bedroom.

CHAPTER EIGHTEEN

'WHAT'S with the sheet all of a sudden?' Ryan demanded to know as he strode towards the bed. 'I thought we'd got past that.' His hand reached out to grab the sheet out of her grasp, flinging it aside before bending to scoop her up into his arms.

Ooh, the feeling of being held naked against him; it was delicious. And so very exciting. Already she wanted him to make love to her again.

'I've run us both a bath,' he said as he carried her into the bathroom. 'Don't bother saying no. It's way too late for you to start being coy.'

She didn't say no—not to the bath. Or what he did to her once they were in the bath. She surrendered herself totally to his wishes, letting him wash her, caress her and position her this way and that so he had the easiest access to every erogenous zone she owned. His touch never seemed crude, yet he took liberties with her body which she'd never allowed before. And, whilst she was quickly desperate for another climax, she didn't come. A combination of his seeming to know when to stop doing whatever it was he was doing just in time, plus his telling her that if she held on until he was inside her again her pleasure would be greatly magnified.

So she held on, despite experiencing a level of frustration previously unknown to her. Constant caresses had extended her nipples to almost painful peaks, where even the slightest touch on them made her gasp. Her stomach was rock-hard with tension, her thighs aching and her sex dying to be filled. Every time his fingers slipped inside her down there, her internal muscles would grasp them tightly whilst her swollen clitoris throbbed with need.

'Ryan, please, I can't stand any more!' she cried at last when it all became too much to bear.

She was straddled across his thighs at the time, their bodies together like two spoons, Ryan's knowing hand rubbing a wet cake of soap back and forth across her burning nipples whilst his erection lay like an armed torpedo along the crease of her buttocks.

He could destroy me if he wanted to, Laura realised with real alarm. Make me ready and willing to do anything he wanted. She understood, suddenly, why that client of his had become obsessed with him. Ryan was the kind of lover who could easily obsess a woman.

Relief swamped Laura when he put aside the cake of soap and lifted her gently from the bath. She was so overcome with gratitude that tears pricked at her eyes. Only fear that he would stop making love to her altogether kept her emotions in check but it was a struggle, especially when he started drying her so sweetly and tenderly. Because by then she didn't want him being sweet and tender with her. All she wanted was for him to carry her back to bed and ravage her.

'What a pity,' he said as he rubbed the ends of her hair dry, 'That we only have that one condom left.'

She could not have agreed more, but couldn't bring herself to say anything so bold. Or so telling.

'Do you like oral sex?' he added, his eyes holding hers.

Laura swallowed. 'I...I can't say that I do.'

Brad hadn't been into anything but straight sex of the hard and fast kind. Mario, however, had been older and more experienced—or so she'd imagined at the time. He'd also been mad about blow jobs. She'd given him what he wanted because she'd loved him, and had thought he loved her; he'd said it often enough. But she'd never liked doing it.

'Why's that?' Ryan said. 'Most girls love it.'

'Do they?'

'The ones I've been with seemed to. Perhaps because I love doing it so much. Would you like me to try to change your mind?'

Laura finally realised he was talking about performing oral sex on her, not the other way around. Now this *was* alien territory for her. Brad had never ventured to suggest such a thing, neither had Mario. When she'd brought the subject up once, he'd said it was demeaning for a real man to do that. She'd believed him because she hadn't liked doing it herself. Now here was a real man claiming he loved it.

'I can see I've sparked your curiosity on the subject,' Ryan said, smiling a smugly satisfied smile. 'Come on, let's give it a whirl.'

'A whirl' was the right word for it. Within seconds he had her back on the bed, his lips creating havoc within her as they traversed her body at the speed of light from her mouth to her breasts, her navel and finally the smooth mound of skin which lay perilously close to her agonisingly aroused sex. She grasped great clumps of sheets in each hand as he came closer and closer to that spot that was screaming for attention. And then he was there, not kissing her, but licking the swollen nub of flesh like a ravenous cat lapping a saucer of cream. Immediately, her back arched from the bed as her body raced blindly towards the edge of the abyss like some crazed lemming.

Immediately, he stopped, lifting his head so that their eyes could meet. Hers were wide whilst his seemed perversely calm.

'Not so quick, Laura,' he told her. 'It'll be better if you wait a while.'

'But I don't want to wait!' she cried out in despair.

He laughed. 'But I'm going to make you wait, my darling.'

'I am not *your darling*,' she snapped, feeling angry with him, and even more fiercely frustrated than she had in the bath.

'I thought you said you didn't like oral sex,' he went on, propping himself up beside her and teasing her breasts mercilessly with wickedly knowing fingers.

'I was referring to fellatio,' she bit out, trying not to groan. But it was hell, the way he now tugged at one of her nipples. Not roughly, she had to admit. But still…

'Ah,' he said, the tugging changing to a slow, twisting motion. 'Well, that is a different matter entirely. But I would imagine a girl of your intelligence would enjoy the sense of power that fellatio would give you. Wouldn't you like to see me squirm as I'm making you squirm at this moment? Wouldn't you like to make me lose control? Think of it as the ultimate triumph over me. Because I can promise you this, lovely Laura—I won't be as cool or as calm as I am at this moment. For those few mad moments, I will be totally yours. Now, isn't that an appealing thought?'

Laura stared up at him. *God, yes.* But it also presented her with a not so appealing thought.

'Is that why you agreed to sleep with me tonight?' she threw at him. 'To triumph over me?'

His fingers stilled on her breast, his eyes becoming thoughtful. 'I have to confess that sleeping with you has given me great satisfaction. And great pleasure. But triumph? No, I can't say that was my train of thought, though you would present a tantalising challenge to any red-blooded man. From the moment you told me what you wanted, however, my main goal tonight has been to give you the kind of sexual pleasure which it's obvious you've never had. Clearly, the man who hurt you was a complete incompetent in the bedroom. I can only imagine he was very young and inexperienced himself.'

'No,' she told him. 'Mario wasn't young at all. Brad was, though.'

'Who the hell is Brad?'

'My first lover. He was a fellow law student who pretended to love me so that he could have free room and board. I found out the truth when I came home one day and found him in bed with someone else.'

'Charming. And the dastardly Mario? Why did he pretend to love you?'

Laura was truly taken aback. 'How do you know that's what he did?'

'Didn't take a genius to figure that one out. All I need to know is why? No, don't tell me, I can guess—he was a client of yours, wasn't he? Right. He was on trial for something sticky and he wanted his defence lawyer to pull out all stops to get him off. Who better than a woman who loved him?'

Laura shook her head. 'I think you *are* a genius.'

He smiled. 'If you say so. So what was he on trial for?'

'Tax evasion. If he'd lost, it would have cost him millions.'

'But he didn't lose, did he? You won the case for him.'

Laura sighed. 'Yes.'

'And then he dropped you.'

'Like a hot cake.' Looking back, she could see that Mario had been a sadist of the first order. He'd enjoyed telling her outside the court house that he'd used her. Enjoyed seeing her hurt and humiliated. At least Brad hadn't been that wicked. He'd looked quite guilty when she'd found him in bed with that girl. Guilt was something Mario would never feel. He was totally conscienceless.

Laura hadn't been at all sad when she'd heard last year that Mario had finally ended up in jail. As for Brad… She'd heard over the legal grapevine that he was considered unemployable as a lawyer after having been fired a couple of times for 'questionable' behaviour. Leopards didn't change their spots, it seemed, something Laura would have to remember about the man she was currently in bed with.

'It's no wonder you went into sexual hibernation,' Ryan said. 'But their loss is my gain. I have to confess that I haven't had this much fun with a woman in years.'

'Fun!' she exclaimed, not sure if she should feel flattered or flattened. Calling sex with her 'fun' was hardly romantic. But then she didn't want him to romance her, did she?

Not really. But she didn't much like him calling what they were doing 'fun'. It seemed demeaning. 'Sex for you is just a game, isn't it?' she threw at him.

'Now, Laura, don't go getting all hoity-toity on me. I've just shown you that great sex does not have to have any connection with love. Not that being in love ever gave *you* great sex in the past,' he pointed out somewhat ruthlessly.

'Sex, my sweet, can be indulged in strictly for pleasure, without the complications which emotional involvement inevitably brings. But I wouldn't say I think of sex as a game. More of a wonderfully satisfying pastime, one where the degree of pleasure involved improves with time and practice.

'Let me assure you that over the years I have devoted much time and practice to perfecting my skills in the bedroom. Trust me when I say that there's so much more that I can show you, and do with you. As I said earlier, one night is not going to be enough. If you'll agree, I'd like to continue our affair when we go back to Sydney. After all, we've crossed the line now; we might as well take full advantage and thoroughly enjoy ourselves.'

Laura stared up at him. Dear heaven, but he was as good a seducer with words as he was with his body. Such thinking reminded her suddenly of Brad and Mario, who'd both had silver tongues. Looking back, she saw that they'd seduced her more with what they'd said than what they'd done. Why had she fallen for their lies about loving her so readily? she wondered now. *Why?*

Because she'd *wanted* to be loved so very, very much. Because she'd been an emotionally needy little fool.

They hadn't even been good lovers. Just good liars.

At least Ryan was a good lover and, though persuasive, he wasn't a liar.

His head dipped to nuzzle at an earlobe, making her shiver uncontrollably.

'Do you agree, lovely Laura?' he whispered in a low, incredibly sexy voice.

What else could she do but nod?

'In that case,' he went on after reaching for their

last condom, 'I think we've done enough waiting for tonight.'

Laura thought the first time he'd made love to her had been incredible. But there was something even more magical the second time round. He took his time once he'd entered her, setting up a slow, sensual rhythm with his hips, his eyes holding hers. Her mouth fell open as the tension built and built, her breathing becoming fast and shallow. Yet there was no anxiety in her, only the warm, sweet pleasure of his flesh rocking back and forth within hers. At no point did she fear she might not come because she knew she would. And when she did he came too, their bodies in perfect physical harmony with each other.

Laura found the experience quite overwhelming. Sexually, they seemed made for each other. But as she clung to him, their bodies still pulsing as one, she realised that emotionally they were as different as chalk and cheese. Laura accepted that at this point in time all she wanted from Ryan was more great sex. But she suspected that if she kept up this level of physical intimacy for too long she would probably fall in love with him. For that was how she was made.

Life was very cruel, Laura decided ruefully,

always to make her attracted to men who would never give her what she wanted.

But at least this time she knew the nature of the beast in advance. Ryan wasn't trying to fool her in any way, shape or form. All he was offering her was a strictly sexual relationship, without caring or commitment of any kind. And, whilst Laura still could not understand why he was so adverse to love and marriage, she had to accept that that was how he was made. There was no point in becoming upset over it. If she wanted to keep experiencing what she'd just experienced, she would have to accept him on his terms, without hoping for anything more.

Of course, it meant risking her heart again and her happiness. But it was impossible to walk away from what Ryan was offering. Already she was addicted to the excitement he engendered in her, the wild pleasures he gave her, not to mention the fabulous orgasms which seemed to last for ever. Her body was still throbbing. And so was his.

She sighed a deliciously sensual sigh.

'I'll be back in a moment, Laura,' he murmured at last before gently disengaging her arms and legs from his back and waist.

She groaned, her limbs going to jelly as they

flopped back onto the bed. A languor had suddenly taken hold of her whole body. Her brain too. She didn't want to fall asleep, didn't want this night to end. But as soon as Ryan left the bed Laura rolled over onto her side and fell fast asleep.

Ryan smiled wryly when he returned to the bed and found Laura out like a light. So much for his erotic plans for the rest of the night.

Though perhaps it was just as well. He too was weary. It had been a long day. A strange day. Who would have believed that it would end with his sleeping with Laura? Even more strange that he would enjoy it so damned much. Ryan pulled some bedclothes over her before getting back into bed, careful not to disturb her. He didn't want to wake her now. He wanted to think, a much easier process when he wasn't aroused. Or, worse, frustrated.

It didn't take Ryan long to figure out that he'd probably made a big mistake tonight. Not only was Laura a work colleague, but she was nothing like the hard-hearted career woman he'd always believed her to be. If she had been, he'd have no worries about continuing his affair with her. Unfortunately, underneath the tough-girl façade she wore seemingly with ease, Laura was actually a sweetie. And a softie. And sexy as hell!

Which was where the real problem lay: Laura's sexiness was different from the kind of sexiness Ryan usually went for. He liked his women a little wild and wanton. Very experienced, too. Liked them to know their way around a man's body. He never went for the shy, retiring types who needed seducing on every level. And he never, God forbid, took a virgin to bed.

Not that Laura was a virgin. But she might as well have been, from what he'd seen tonight. Perversely, he'd loved that about her, loved it that she was so inexperienced. Her responses to the things he'd done were wonderfully fresh, full of surprise and the most enchanting gratitude—not to mention passion. Her orgasms had been very intense.

It irked Ryan considerably that Laura had loved not one but two total bastards in her life. But then, that was the nature of love, wasn't it? It didn't make sense. It was both irrational and sometimes self-destructive, in his opinion, especially where women were concerned.

Which brought him to his major problem where Laura was concerned.

What if she fell in love with him?

There was no use pretending that it couldn't happen, just because Laura didn't overly like him. Women fell in love with men they didn't like all the time.

Ryan didn't want to hurt her. Hell, he'd spent most of his life trying not to hurt women. Not that he'd always succeeded. But he had never deliberately set out to hurt any of them.

Would he hurt Laura if he continued sleeping with her?

That was the question he had to answer before morning came. Which meant before he surrendered to his own tiredness and dropped off to sleep.

Ryan frowned. Maybe he would hurt her more if he stopped. Clearly, she'd loved the sex tonight. Loved it all. If he called it quits tomorrow morning she might think she'd done something wrong, or that he'd already grown bored with her. She would take it as a personal rejection. Women were quick to blame themselves when a man dumped them. To do so after just one night together would be cruel.

On top of that, there was no guarantee that Laura would become emotionally involved with him. She was thirty years old and a lawyer, for pity's sake. Hardly a naïve little thing. She already knew the score where he was concerned, knew that he was not husband material. All he was good for was some fun and games, something which she was in dire need of, in his opinion.

If she continued to sleep with him, then the risk was hers, wasn't it? Her future happiness was not his responsibility. She was an adult who could decide for herself what she wanted to do. He wasn't about to force her to continue their affair. It was up to her. But he would ask her again in the morning if that was what she wanted. Give her a chance to change her mind.

Feeling marginally better, Ryan stretched out and closed his eyes. But they immediately snapped open again. Of course, if Laura did decide to continue their affair—and he was pretty sure that she would—he would have to get himself a new lawyer. He would make that very clear indeed.

Never mixing business with pleasure was one rule Ryan didn't intend to break!

CHAPTER NINETEEN

RYAN woke before Laura. Without thinking, he snuggled up to her still sleeping form, curving his body around hers from behind. His arousal was instantaneous and extremely corrupting, banishing any thought of giving her either the opportunity or the time to change her mind about continuing their sexual relationship. Already he was stroking her bare breasts, stirring her back to consciousness, wallowing in the way she started moaning with pleasure.

And then he remembered—no more condoms.

Swearing with frustration, he leapt out of the bed and marched off to the bathroom where he jumped into a cold shower, staying there till he was ready to behave himself. By the time he emerged, well wrapped in a towel, Laura was wide awake and sitting up in the bed, a sheet thankfully clutched over those beautiful breasts of hers.

'Sorry about that,' he muttered, striding over to

the wardrobe where his clothes were hung. 'Forgot we'd run out of protection.'

Laura was sorry too—sorry that he'd stopped.

'The bathroom's all yours,' he threw over his shoulder. 'Though I'll have to go back and shave at some stage. I'd leave the stubble on today in other circumstances, but I have a suspicion that Cynthia would not approve. Or your gran, for that matter.'

'You're probably right about Aunt Cynthia, but Gran won't mind. She likes macho-looking men.'

Me too, Laura thought as she admired Ryan's back view. She loved the wideness of his shoulders and the narrowness of his waist and hips. Loved the rippling muscles which framed his spine and bulged in his arms. Loved the length and strength of his legs.

He shrugged those gorgeously broad shoulders. 'In that case I won't bother.'

She stayed to watch him dress, even though she really needed to go to the bathroom. But she held on long enough to see him step into some sexy Y-fronts then pull on the black jeans he'd worn yesterday. A white T-shirt followed, over which he drew on a long-sleeved black shirt. What was it about a man in black, she wondered, that was so darned sexy?

He turned suddenly, his eyes thoughtful. 'Before I forget, there's something I have to ask you.'

Laura's heart contracted with immediate anxiety. 'Oh? What?'

'Are you quite sure you want to keep sleeping with me? If you would prefer to leave things as a one-night stand, I'll understand.'

Laura was truly taken aback, and a little dismayed. Was this his way of saying he wanted out?

She could only shake her head. 'I don't understand you, Ryan. I thought you still wanted me this morning.'

'I do.'

'Then what's the problem all of a sudden?'

'No problem on my part. I just wanted to give you the chance to change your mind. Sometimes things appear differently the morning after the night before. One's thoughts become clearer.'

'My thoughts are quite clear, thank you very much,' she said somewhat tartly. She hated it when men acted as though women were silly creatures who didn't know their own mind.

'You do realise that becoming my lover is not a permanent position,' he went on firmly. 'And that it will mean the end of our business relationship.'

Laura was beginning to become quite impatient

with him. There really was no need to keep reminding her what the score was. She already knew
his track record.

'That's fine by me,' she bit out. 'I too have a life
rule about having affairs with clients.'

His eyebrows lifted. 'Ah yes. I'd forgotten for a
moment that you'd done that before. But of course
you were in love with that particular client. Which
is why it ended badly.'

The penny finally dropped for Laura. 'Oh, I see.
You're worried that I might fall in love with you?'

'Something like that.'

'You truly are a most arrogant man.'

'Possibly,' he admitted. 'But not, thankfully, a
libertine.'

'That's debatable at this point in time.'

He smiled. 'I rather like it when you get stroppy.'

'That's because it makes you feel safe!' she
snapped.

He laughed. 'Nothing about you right now makes
me feel safe, Laura. Which is why I want you to
get that beautiful body of yours into the bathroom
where I can't get at it.'

Laura tried to stay annoyed with him—but how
could she when he'd just called her beautiful, not

to mention admitted to an almost uncontrollable desire for her?

'You'll have to turn away then,' she told him with feigned haughtiness. 'I wouldn't want you to lose control at the sight of my beautiful *naked* body.'

His groan secretly delighted her. 'Must you remind me? Okay then,' he added as he spun round to put his back to her. 'Get going. And take some bloody clothes with you!'

'I can't. They're over there where you are.'

'In that case just get yourself into that bathroom the way you are. But I won't be here when you come out. I'll be downstairs somewhere, chatting up Cynthia!'

Ryan breathed a sigh of relief once Laura was safely in the bathroom. She hadn't been far wrong with her caustic remark about his losing control at the sight of her nakedness. He'd done his best to sound calm and reasonable when he'd given her the chance to change her mind—and when he'd reminded her that any relationship with him was never a permanent one. But underneath his cool exterior, he'd been struggling all the while to ignore the less-than-cool messages his body kept sending him.

He wasn't sure what he would have done if she'd

said no, Ryan, I don't want to have any more sex with you. He suspected his behaviour at that point in time might not have been very noble. Only the knowledge that he could take her to bed tonight and on many more future nights had put some sanity into his head and some control over his wayward flesh.

Ryan shook his head as he sat down to put on his socks and shoes. It had been a long time since a woman had got under his skin the way Laura had. Actually, he could not remember it happening before at all. Ever!

Any other man might have imagined he was falling in love but Ryan knew differently. Romantic love was not an emotion he was capable of, not since he'd seen up close and personally what that kind of love had done to his mother. Ryan had only been twelve when he'd vowed never to fall in love, or marry, or have children. And nothing had happened since to change his mind on that score.

So, no, he knew he wasn't in love with Laura. It was desire which was possessing him at the moment, a desire which was heightened by her lack of sexual experience. He could not wait to show her everything. Tonight simply could not come quickly enough!

CHAPTER TWENTY

'THANK God you rang me,' were Alison's first words. 'I've been dying of curiosity all morning.'

'It's only ten-thirty,' Laura told her friend. 'I couldn't ring you before. I haven't had a minute to myself.'

A white lie, actually. She'd been alone upstairs for a good while before breakfast but had spent the time trying to get her head around things. As soon as Ryan had left the room and she'd been out of his corrupting presence, Laura had been besieged by doubt over what she'd agreed to.

So much for her much-vaunted pride! She felt disgusted with herself, not so much for sleeping with him last night—wild horses could not have stopped her from doing that!—but for agreeing to sleep with him some more without his offering her anything in return. He'd not even offered her the face-saving grace of becoming a proper girl-friend. He hadn't said a word about dating her, just about sex.

On top of that he expected her to waltz into work and announce that he was no longer her client? What excuse could she possibly give? 'Sorry but he's screwing me now and he doesn't screw women he works with'?

The man wanted his cake and wanted to eat it too, came the mutinous thought.

The trouble was she still wanted him on *any* terms. The shock and shame of this realisation was almost too much to bear.

She'd had to force herself to go downstairs for breakfast and to face not just Ryan but the rest of the family. She'd found them all in the kitchen being treated to one of Aunt Cynthia's over-the-top English-style breakfasts. Laura was never one for eating anything heavy in the mornings and would usually have refused, but this time she'd allowed herself to be fed bacon, eggs, baked beans and fried tomatoes with lashings of toast, because that way she hadn't had to talk much.

After breakfast, she'd helped her aunt wash up whilst Ryan had whisked Jane off on the promised drive in his convertible. He still hadn't returned half an hour later, which had given Laura the opportunity to go upstairs and finally ring her friend.

'You sound a little strained,' Alison said. 'Please

don't tell me that nothing happened last night between you two?'

'Something happened all right.'

'Ooh. Do tell.'

Laura told her everything. Well, not in minute detail, but in broad strokes; some things were too private to divulge. And possibly too embarrassing. But she certainly told her every single thing about the chat Ryan had had with her when she had woken up, plus her decision to continue her affair with Ryan even though she knew it was heading nowhere.

'Please don't tell me I'm a fool,' she finished up, feeling drained all of a sudden.

'Far from it,' Alison said. 'If I were in your position I'd do exactly the same.'

'You would?'

'Yes, of course! After all, Laura, what's your alternative? You crawl back into an even more bitter and frustrated spinster cave where you hate all men and never have any fun?'

'But what if I fall in love with him, Alison?' she cried, voicing the worst fear she had about the situation. 'I can't afford to fall for another Mr Wrong. I just can't!'

'But this is different to the other two. Can't you

see that? They pretended they loved you. Ryan wants nothing from you but your body.'

'But that sounds so cheap and nasty!'

'Not to me, it doesn't. To me it sounds seriously sexy. Go for it, I say. And, if you fall in love with him, so what? You might be sad for a while when it's over, but you won't be left feeling bitter and betrayed. You'll have some wonderful memories of a great lover who's made you see how beautiful and sexy you are. And, who knows? You might turn out to be the one.'

'What one?'

'The one who changes his mind about love and marriage.'

Laura laughed. 'You don't know Ryan.'

'Maybe not, but I'd like to. Why don't you bring him over next weekend for a barbeque?'

'I don't think he wants that kind of relationship.'

'You mean he just wants sex from you and nothing else?' Now Alison sounded shocked. 'No dates or anything like that?'

'I think so.'

'Now, that *is* cheap and nasty. You wouldn't settle for that, Laura? Surely?'

'That's what I'm afraid of, Alison. That I might settle for *any* arrangement with him.'

'Oh dear...'

'What do you mean by saying "oh dear" like that?'

Alison stopped herself just in time from telling her friend that it sounded like she was already in love with him. Nothing was to be gained by telling her, if that was the case.

But she had an awful feeling that this affair was not going to turn out well for Laura. There was nothing to be gained by telling her that, either. She was damned if she did, and damned if she didn't.

'I just don't like the thought of your agreeing to anything, Laura,' she said instead. 'Don't lose your pride over the man, no matter how good he is in bed.'

'A minute ago you were all for my having more sex with him!' Laura exclaimed, sounding exasperated.

'I am. Truly. Just...be careful.'

Suddenly, she wished she hadn't encouraged Laura to go to bed with him.

'I have to go, Alison. I can hear Ryan's car coming up the drive.'

'Ring me tonight, will you?'

'Maybe not till tomorrow,' Laura returned. 'I might be busy tonight.'

Of course, Alison thought sourly. *The lord and master of the bedroom will want another dose of what he'd obviously enjoyed last night.* And Alison knew what that was—relative innocence. That was what intrigued him about Laura, came the sudden, highly intuitive realisation. She wasn't like all the other Penthouse Pet types that playboys usually bedded. She was a lovely sincere girl with a warm heart who hadn't slept around, and who was way too vulnerable for the likes of Ryan Armstrong.

Alison grimaced as she wished she could take back all the stupid advice she'd given Laura, both yesterday and today. She should have realised that her friend wasn't cut out for strictly sexual flings. She was going to get hurt again and she, Alison, would be partly responsible. But it was too late now. The die had been cast and Laura would just have to roll with it. All Alison could do was be there when the end came.

But she wasn't looking forward to it.

CHAPTER TWENTY-ONE

'YOUR family's not that bad, Laura,' were Ryan's first words as they drove away from the house.

Laura sighed. 'They were greatly improved this weekend,' she admitted. 'But that was because of your influence. You had Gran eating out of your hand over lunch. What on earth did you say to her during that drive? She seemed much brighter than yesterday.'

'I hardly said a word; she did most of the talking. Told me where to drive. I just followed orders. She showed me the village and the church, the one near the Hunter Valley gardens. By the way, she said to tell you that that was where she wanted her funeral service to be held.'

'Oh, for pity's sake!'

'She wasn't being maudlin, Laura. Just practical.'

'But she won't die now. Not for ages. What else did she say? She didn't drop any hints about our getting engaged, did she?'

'Not directly. Though she did point out that they use that church for a lot weddings as well.'

'And what did you say to that?'

'Nothing, that I recall.'

'You must have said something to make her look so pleased with you.'

'I did promise to come to her eightieth-birthday party in November.'

'Oh no. Do you think that was a good idea?'

'I don't see why not.'

'Well, I mean, we might not last that long.' Laura's conversation with Alison had made her determined not to get any silly female hopes up where Ryan was concerned.

His sharp sideways glance startled her. 'My girl-friends usually last more than two months, Miss Cynical.'

Laura tried to remain looking cool but it was difficult when her heart had just turned over with a ridiculous burst of happiness. 'You mean you want to make our relationship a public one?'

Now he looked quite annoyed. 'Well, of course I do! What had you been envisaging? That I would keep you as some dirty little secret? Why on earth would I do that?'

Laura knew she couldn't tell him the truth—that

she'd been imagining just that. 'I guess because I'm not the kind of gorgeous, glamorous female that you usually date,' she said instead.

'Good God, Laura, did you get a look at yourself last night? You are just as gorgeous and glamorous-looking as any of my previous girlfriends.'

'But I don't usually look like that on a day-to-day basis, as you well know.'

'There's no reason why you can't. All you have to do is go shopping for some more new clothes and wear a bit of make-up occasionally.'

'People at work will wonder what's happened to me.'

'So? Do you honestly care what they think?'

'Yes, I do,' she admitted. The end result of such a radical makeover was slowly sinking in. She didn't want her colleagues laughing at her behind her back. She would look a complete fool if she went in there all glammed up and told them Ryan could no longer be her client because she was dating him. They all knew what he was like. The women there had often made caustic remarks about his being a serial lady-killer.

'No, Ryan,' she said firmly, surprising herself.

He slanted her a startled glance. 'No *what*?'

'No, I don't want to buy a whole new wardrobe and, no, I don't want to be your girlfriend.'

The sudden silence inside the car was electric with unspoken tension. She saw his knuckles go white as he gripped the steering wheel; saw his shoulders rise.

'You don't mean that,' he said at last, his tone one of sheer disbelief.

'But I do.'

'You don't want to sleep with me any more?'

'I didn't say that.'

His head whipped round, shock written all over his face. Laura was pretty shocked herself—at herself, for voicing out loud what had suddenly entered her head. That it was *he* she wanted to keep as *her* dirty little secret, not the other way round.

When his car drifted dangerously close to the lane next to them—and the truck which was rumbling along at high speed—Ryan quickly returned his attention to his driving, swearing volubly as he righted the car, slowing down appreciably before he spoke again.

'You can't be seriously suggesting what I think you're suggesting,' he bit out, obviously not happy with being cast in the role of her secret lover.

Now that the initial shock of her suggestion had

worn off, Laura found herself quite taken with the idea. How better to protect herself from future hurt and humiliation than by keeping their affair strictly sexual and, yes, totally secret? Not to mention brief. No one knew better than Laura that time and sustained intimacy—even that of a strictly sexual nature—would ultimately be her undoing. A week or two should be long enough to burn out a good degree of the lust that was still plaguing her, she decided. Long enough too to satisfy her curiosity over all those wildly erotic things Ryan claimed he could show her.

'It would be the best solution all round,' she said, feeling strangely exhilarated at having taken control of her destiny. 'You're a great lover, Ryan. Possibly the best I'll ever have in my lifetime. Which is why I want to sample some more of your incredible talent in the bedroom.

'But we both know you won't ever give me what I really want—which is a husband and a family. Added to that is the fact that I'm not getting any younger. Frankly, becoming your girlfriend, even for a few months, is a waste of my valuable time.

'The truth is I just want to have some more sex with you, but not for too long. A couple of weeks should do the trick. I appreciate my somewhat radical proposal might be a blow to your ego, but think of the plus side—you won't have to take me out anywhere or buy me expensive dinners. You won't have to meet my friends. All you have to do is—'

'Don't you dare use that word!' Ryan broke in savagely.

Laura found his outrage extremely hypocritical, something which he said he despised. 'I was only going to say *shag*,' she invented. She'd actually been going to say 'make love to me' in a momentary lack of concentration.

'I hate that word too.'

'Lord, but aren't we the sensitive one all of a sudden? And this from a man who had no qualms pointing out to me that all he was good for was sex. What would you prefer to call it then? Bonk? Screw?'

'I would prefer that you agreed to become my girlfriend for real!' he snapped.

Laura's back teeth clenched together hard in her jaw, as the temptation to say yes was almost overwhelming.

'Sorry,' she bit out. 'No can do.'

'*Sorry?*' he retorted, throwing her a savage glance. 'I don't think you're sorry at all.'

'And I think you should keep your eyes on the road,' she said when the car drifted once again.

He swore, using the four-letter word he hadn't wanted her to say. He didn't apologise, however. Instead, he fell silent and sped up, the car eating up the miles as only a powerful sports car could. Laura fell stubbornly silent too, determined not to weaken in her resolve to retain control of her life and this affair. They'd crossed the Hawkesbury River Bridge and were drawing near the outer suburbs of Sydney before Ryan spoke again.

'Right,' he said abruptly. 'Now that I've calmed down, this is the way I see the situation. I'm sorry if I gave you the impression that all I want from you is sex. I like you, Laura. Like your company and your conversation. I would enjoy taking you places and buying you expensive dinners. I would especially enjoy seeing you throw off that ridiculously tough façade you've been hiding behind and become the warm, beautiful, sexy, sophisticated woman which I know you could be.

'As for my wasting your valuable time, I don't believe any time you spend with me would be a waste. Life should not always be lived for the future, but sometimes for the here and now.'

He paused for a long moment, perhaps waiting

for his quite seductive argument to work its magic on her. But Laura wasn't at all convinced. She did not believe in that live-for-the-moment rubbish. Unless fate stepped in with an unfortunately terminal accident or disease, the future inevitably arrived, during which you had to live with what you'd done in the past. It was all right for him; he didn't fall in love. But she did! And she wasn't going to. Not this time!

'I see,' he said with a rueful glance at her unmoved face. 'Obviously what I believe is irrelevant. Look, I'm not in the business of trying to change a woman's mind. But neither am I going to agree to such a ridiculous scheme. At the same time, I still want you, Laura—with a rather irrational desire, I am discovering. So I will stay with you tonight and endeavour to give you lots of the only thing you want from me. But, come tomorrow morning, that will be that. Our ways will part, never to be crossed again. That's my counter proposal. If you don't agree, then I'm afraid it will be quits today at your door.'

Laura sucked in sharply, her emotions in immediate disarray. So much for her façade of cool control!

Fury that he'd accused her of callously using

him mingled with panic at the possibility that she would never be with him again. Which would be the case if she didn't agree to his 'counter proposal'. But how *could* she agree now? He'd already made her sound like some sex-crazed fool who'd thrown away any chance of a real relationship in exchange for a fortnight's sex. To agree to just one night of the same seemed so much worse.

She wasn't *that* desperate, was she?

'I'm sorry you think so badly of me,' she said, her voice sounding calm despite a trembling starting deep inside. 'I was just trying to be honest with you with my proposal, and not hypocritical. I don't think you can blame me for suggesting a sex-only affair when you yourself said you couldn't offer me any form of commitment. But I can see now that such an arrangement won't work for me, even for one more night. It is far better that we call it quits today, then you can move on the way you say you always do, and so will I. Hopefully, the next time I find a man I fancy, he'll want more than a temporary relationship.'

Ryan clenched his teeth down hard in his jaw as he listened to her quite stunning rejection of his proposal. And there he'd been, thinking she would not dare knock him back, not when she'd virtually admitted she was mad for him. He'd imagined that he'd backed her into a corner where he'd be the one in control and she would come begging for more. Which was what he wanted—more of Laura, naked and willing, in his arms. But on his terms, not hers. A man did have his pride.

Unfortunately, pride did have its downside. *He* was the one backed into a corner now. And there'd be no begging from *his* corner.

'Fine,' he bit out. 'We'll call it quits today.'

It was like a physical blow to Laura. She struggled not to cry out, then not to cry. Oh God, what had she done? Suddenly even one night with him was better than this…this emptiness.

'I will leave it up to you to arrange for another lawyer to be sent to me every Friday afternoon,' he went on, his voice sounding bitter. 'I don't care what excuse you give.'

'All right,' she said, her own voice sounding bleak.

'Now, if you don't mind, I don't want to talk any more.' And he turned on the radio, at the same time pressing whatever button it took for the roof automatically to go back into place.

Laura's heart sank. The roof closing was like a sign that everything was over. *They* were over.

She turned her face away towards the passenger window so Ryan couldn't see the tears filling her eyes.

CHAPTER TWENTY-TWO

IT STARTED to rain not long after they left the motorway, a grey drizzle which reflected the condition of Laura's emotions. She ached to say something to take away the horribly strained silence which had permeated the car since their argument, but could not seem to find the courage to speak up.

Or was it common sense keeping her quiet?

If she were brutally honest, Laura suspected that if she opened her mouth she would start apologising wildly, then agreeing to whatever Ryan wanted just so that he wouldn't drop her at her door. The thought of never seeing him again was appalling, so appalling that she began to wonder if she'd already fallen in love with him. It seemed unlikely, but why else would she feel so devastated? Surely it couldn't still be just lust driving her feelings?

But, even as she speculated on the reason behind her despair, her eyes slid over to where Ryan's hands were wrapped around the steering wheel. His hands were large, with long, strong fingers which had no doubt helped make him become a success as a goalkeeper. But none of that mattered to Laura. All she could think about when she looked at his hands was how gentle they'd been on her. Gentle, yet knowing. They'd explored all her orifices with stunning intimacy. She could feel them now, inside her, stroking, teasing, arousing.

Oh God, she thought as her body was suddenly overwhelmed by the most intense longing; her belly tightened as did her nipples. *At least now I know*, she thought wildly as hot blood roared around her veins, flushing her cheeks and making her break out into strangely chilling goose-bumps. Not love—still just lust.

She almost died of shame when he glanced over at her at that precise moment. It was impossible to hide the telling evidence of her flaming face. Impossible to look anything but what she was: desperate for him.

Yet he didn't say a single word. He just stared at her for a long moment before returning his attention to the road. But she saw that his knuckles had whitened, and she could feel an answering tension in him. He knew what she wanted, and he wanted the same thing.

Not a word was spoken when he pulled up outside her house. They climbed out in the most appalling silence. Ryan helped her to carry her things up onto the front porch. Rambo didn't make an appearance, which surprised her. Possibly he was curled up asleep in the neighbour's rocking chair which was something he liked to do when she was away. She was left to fumble with her keys. Once the door was open, she turned to face Ryan, terrified that he would still leave, and equally terrified that he wouldn't.

'Ryan, I—'

'Just shut up,' he broke in, his face and eyes tormented as he dropped everything he was holding onto the verandah and pushed her inside the hallway, kicking the door shut behind him.

There was no question of fighting him, or even protesting, because she wanted him to do what it was obvious he was going to do. The trembling had already started inside. The trembling and the wild, uncontrollable excitement.

Yes, yes, slam me up against the wall, she urged silently as he did exactly that. *Kiss me till I can't think. Rip my clothes off. Ravish me.*

'God help me!' she cried out when he finally surged up into her.

It was a manic mating; raw, rough and totally beyond reason. Beyond everything in this world which smacked of common sense and control.

And she revelled in it, her mouth gasping wide as he plundered her depths with the most primal passion. He came first, the fierce spasms of his flesh triggering her own cataclysmic climax. Laura's release was so intense, so overwhelming, that she started to sob afterwards, tears streaming down her face as her arms flopped down by her side and her legs went to jelly. She might have slid down to the floor if Ryan's body hadn't been holding her up.

'Oh God, Laura,' he groaned, then clasped her tightly to him. 'I'm so sorry. So dreadfully sorry.'

'It… It's all right…' she somehow managed to stammer between sobs.

'No,' he said, taking her by the shoulders as he levered his body away from hers, his abrupt withdrawal bringing a startled gasp from her lungs. His eyes when they met hers were haunted. 'It's not all right. What I did just now… It was all wrong.'

His distress forced her to get control of her weeping so she could reassure him that he hadn't raped her, if that was what he was thinking. She'd been with him all the way. She could have struggled, could have said no, but she hadn't.

'I'm as much to blame as you, Ryan,' she choked out, not quite in control of her voice just yet.

'I can't accept that,' he ground out as he zipped up his jeans then set about helping her with her clothes, which hadn't been properly removed either, just enough to let him have his way with her. 'I forced myself on you. And I didn't use protection. What if you fall pregnant? I should be put up against a wall and shot!'

'You didn't *force* me, Ryan,' she reiterated firmly. 'I have free will and I wanted you to do what you did. I enjoyed it. You know I did.'

He just stared at her.

'Let me assure you that my chances of getting pregnant are negligible,' she went on, thankful that she was one of those girls who kept dates pretty clear in her head—not that her head was all that clear at the moment. 'My period is due on Wednesday and I'm as regular as clockwork. It's a very safe time for me in that regard.

'Unless, of course,' she added, her heart jolting as another not very nice thought came to her, 'You're worried about my catching something far worse than a baby.' There was no use pretending that he wasn't a player with a stream of partners behind him. Maybe he'd done this kind of thing before—had unsafe sex, and with someone not as safe as she was.

He looked genuinely shocked at her enquiry. 'You have my word that your health is at no risk from me. I have never before had unsafe sex. Not once. This is a first for me, believe me.'

'Really?' Laura couldn't help it. She smiled at his admission. There was something perversely flattering that she'd been the one and only woman to make him lose control like that.

'Yes, really, Miss Smug.' He cocked his head on one side and gave her a long thoughtful look. 'I take it, then, that you won't mind if I stay the night?'

'I…er…was actually hoping for more than one night,' she said, well aware that she wasn't strong enough to send him away. Not yet.

Rambo bolting down the hallway towards her was a thankful distraction from the telling heat that was suddenly threatening to engulf her.

'Hi, sweetie,' she said. 'Did you miss me?'

He miaowed once, then sauntered over and rubbed

himself around Ryan's ankles. When Ryan scooped him up into his arms, Rambo began to purr.

'He likes you,' Laura said, trying not to feel jealous.

'He's a very nice cat. Even with only one eye. His fur is incredibly soft.'

'He's very spoiled.'

'I can imagine. Does he sleep on your bed every night?'

'No. He likes to roam at night. I've tried locking him in, but when I do he just sits at the window in my room and cries. It's easier to just let him do what he wants.'

'Smart cat. He's trained you well.'

'I love him,' she said somewhat defensively. 'When you love your pet, you can't bear to see it unhappy, or hurt.'

'Hence the three-thousand-dollar vet bill,' Ryan said.

Laura refused to be irked by the dry amusement in his voice. 'I would have spent ten thousand dollars to keep Rambo alive! Now, if you don't mind, I have to feed him or he'll be a pain later on. And we wouldn't want that, would we?' she threw at him snakily.

He smiled a wry smile. 'Glad to see that some

things about you haven't changed. Here,' he said, and handed the cat over. 'He's all yours. By the way, after you've fed him, is there a chance of some coffee? You pointed the kitchen out to me yesterday.'

Only yesterday? Laura thought with amazement as she carried Rambo down to the kitchen. One short day and so much had changed. The twice-bitten-forever-shy Laura of yesterday would have worried herself sick over where her affair with Ryan was heading. This morning's Laura had still been a little concerned.

The Laura who'd just had wild but fantastic sex up against a wall now looked at things very differently. No longer was she going to worry about falling in love with Ryan and ending up with another broken heart. She was going to embrace the lust which was still raging within her and live for the heat of the moment. The long-term future could go hang itself. The only future she cared about was the immediate future. Which was tonight.

Her heartbeat quickened as she realised that she would soon be back in bed with Ryan. Back in his arms, back experiencing the most incredible pleasure. She could not wait to be totally naked with him once more. To have him touch her everywhere. To touch him everywhere as well. Her head swirled at the thought of going down on him. Not reluctantly, but avidly. And certainly not because of some silly idea of sacrificial love. She wanted to feel that power which he'd described to her last night, wanted to make him lose control, all because of *her.*

It was a heady thought. Heady, intoxicating and thrilling.

Rambo's impatient miaow snapped her back to the present.

'You wouldn't understand, Rambo,' she muttered as she went about getting him the special treat she always fed him when she wanted him to settle. 'You've been de-sexed. Now, here, eat up. After which I want you to be a good boy and don't bother me for the rest of the night.'

'I hope you're not talking about me,' Ryan said as he strode into the kitchen, his beautiful blue eyes glittering with amusement. 'Because I don't intend to be good. And I am going to bother you. But not till I've had some coffee. Strong coffee. I suggest you have some as well; don't want you falling asleep on me.' He glanced around. 'I like your kitchen. The wood's a nice colour.'

'It's oak,' Laura said as she dropped the empty tin in the garbage. '*Real* oak.'

'It's classy,' he said, and pulled out one of the two wooden stools which fronted the small breakfast bar. 'Like you,' he added.

Laura wasn't sure what to say to such a compliment, so she settled for a simple, 'Thank you,' before turning away from him to put the kettle on and get everything ready for coffee.

'I only have instant, I'm afraid,' she said as she busied herself with the mugs.

'No problem; I'm not fussy. Just make it black and strong, with no sugar.'

'I don't know how you can bear drinking coffee without milk and sugar.'

'I learned when I had no milk and sugar,' he returned dryly.

She frowned as she turned back to face him. 'Were you really that poor once?'

'You have no idea.'

'No,' she agreed thoughtfully. 'I guess I haven't. I may have been unhappy as a teenager but I was never poor. I certainly never went hungry. That must have been horrible.'

Ryan shrugged, as though he no longer thought about it. Or cared. 'It made me appreciate things once I could afford them. And it made me work hard so that I could afford them. But enough of such talk. I never like talking about the past. It's a waste of time.'

'But the past is what makes you what you are today,' Laura said, curious now to find out more about him. She realised that he'd revealed only scant details about his early life to her family yesterday. Though Gran had picked up on the fact that his childhood couldn't have been easy.

'Yes I do know that, Laura,' he replied a little impatiently. 'But I don't subscribe to analysis of any kind. It does a person no good at all to rake over the past, especially when the things they're raking over are usually wretched and made them miserable. It just sets off old problems again. Far better to put things behind you and move on.'

Laura almost said that was much easier said than done but decided to let the matter drop. She didn't want to say or do anything to spoil the rest of the evening.

'Speaking of moving on,' he added dryly. 'So come with me, woman. Bed awaits.'

CHAPTER TWENTY-THREE

LAURA still fell asleep, but only after a lengthy sexual marathon where they made love over and over and over, in every position Ryan knew, including up against the wall again, though in the shower this time and with Laura facing the wall.

He didn't succumb to sleep, however, despite feeling drained. His mind would not let him rest, plaguing him with the things Laura had said earlier about how much the past influenced the present, and the person one eventually became. As he'd already told Laura, he did actually know that. Ryan understood full well why he avoided love and marriage. Why he avoided emotional involvement of any kind with the opposite sex.

He'd always believed that nothing would ever change that. That no woman alive was capable of unlocking the iron cage he'd fused shut around his heart the day he'd come home from school and found his mother dead on the floor and his father curled up in a corner, sobbing that he hadn't meant to do it, that he loved her.

Ryan had lived a long time since that day— twenty-five years to be exact. Not once in all that time had a woman touched his heart, let alone his soul.

Until now…

Was this love he was finally feeling? He wondered as he frowned down at Laura's sleeping form.

He wasn't sure, since he didn't know what romantic love felt like. All he knew was that sex with Laura was different from anything he'd experienced before. He could not seem to get enough of her. Usually, his desire lessened sharply after a couple of times, his days of wanting sex all night long a thing of the past. Not so with Laura. Already he wanted to feel that special feeling again, the one which jolted him every time he entered her, then grew in intensity, culminating in waves of rapture. He'd never felt anything like it. Hell on earth—would he never be satisfied?

This can't be love, he decided as he rolled over and stared down at her naked bottom with its peach-like buttocks. True love would be less sexually driven. It was still just lust. A more obsessive form than usual, but just lust all the same. Give it time and these cravings would fade.

But not yet, he accepted when he reached out to touch her.

Laura woke to the delicious sensation of Ryan stroking her back. She was lying face down, on the bed, her arms bent upwards, her hands under the pillow that her head was resting on.

'Mmm,' she murmured sleepily, her mind not yet fully awake.

It soon snapped to, however, when his hand abandoned her back and started paying her more intimate attention. Today, she was just all excitement. She'd abandoned embarrassment as a lost cause; Ryan didn't have an embarrassed bone in his body when it came to sex. Everything in his view was natural and healthy, every part of a woman's body put there for his pleasure. And her own.

After a while, however, Laura didn't want to just lie there, letting him do what he was doing—though it was lovely. She wanted to do things to him for a change. With a small moan—it *was* seriously tempting just to stay where she was and let him have his wicked way with her—she rolled over abruptly. Pushing her hair out of her eyes, she sat up and met his somewhat startled eyes.

'You can do that later,' she said breathlessly. 'It's my turn now.'

His eyebrows arched. 'Your turn to do what?'

'Will you please stop talking? Oh my goodness!' she gasped when she pushed him down onto his back and she saw how aroused he already was.

'How long was I asleep?' she asked him in amazement. After all, they'd already made love quite a few times before she had dropped off, including that incredible time in the shower.

'Long enough,' he growled.

'Obviously,' she said, unable to stop herself from reaching out to touch him.

When she encircled him in her hand, he sucked in sharply, sending her eyes to his. This was the one thing she still hadn't done. Up until now it had been all him doing things to her.

'Do you like women going down on you?' she asked him, her voice thick with excitement.

'I do if they do,' he replied, his voice sounding strained. 'You said you didn't—like it, that is.'

'True. But that was before and this is now. I think I *will* like it with you.'

He groaned when she began to bend her head,

groaning again when she put her lips to him in a tender kiss before slowly, ever so slowly, licking the head all over.

She didn't just like doing it, Laura realised dazedly by the time she drew him fully into her mouth. She *loved* it. Loved the feeling, not of power so much, but of knowing how much he was loving it. He'd given her so much pleasure; now it was her turn to give him pleasure. *Lots* of pleasure, by the strangled sounds he was making. She didn't care if he came in her mouth. She wanted him to come. Wanted him to stop struggling for control—which she sensed he was—and just let go. Determined, she picked up the pace, lifting and lowering her head to the rhythm of the thudding drumbeat her own blood was making in her head.

But, just when she was sure he was about to come, he grabbed her and dragged her upwards, his strong hands lifting her up over him then lowering her down so that she was straddled across his hips.

'I want you with me,' he growled. 'Here, put this on me,' he ordered in gravelly tones, shoving a condom into her hands. 'Hurry,' he snapped when she hesitated.

She had a little trouble sliding the protective

sheath over him but managed at last, amazed when he slid inside her with shocking ease, her internal muscles automatically taking hold of him in a vice-like grip.

'Hell on earth, woman,' he choked out, his face twisting.

Laura's face fell. 'Am I hurting you?' This was the first time she'd ever been on top in her life. Mario and Brad had both been the kind of males who would never allow a woman to take the reins during sex. 'I'm sorry. It's just that I…I haven't done it this way before.'

He stared up at her. 'You've never been on top?'

'No. Never. I'm so sorry.'

'There's absolutely no need for you to apologise.'

'But I *hurt* you!'

His smile was rueful. 'There's a fine line between pleasure and pain, Laura. I promise you that what I'm feeling is more pleasure than pain. Now, this is the way,' he said, cupping her buttocks with his large, strong hands and moving her.

She gasped. Oh, how heavenly it felt. She soon didn't need any help, riding him all by herself, faster and faster. His hips began to lift from the bed, pushing him even deeper inside her. She moaned and leant forward, her breasts swinging free of her chest wall, her bottom lifting slightly. Incredibly, the level of her pleasure increased with the change of angle, each forward thrust sending electric shocks charging through her body. Her climax hit with such blinding force that she cried out. Ryan cried out as well, his body spasming wildly within hers. She collapsed across his chest, her head coming to rest over his madly galloping heart.

It was then that she began to weep, her whole body suddenly surrendering to a storm of emotion that she was yet to understand.

'Hush, my darling,' Ryan crooned as he wrapped his arms around her back and held her tightly against him. 'Hush. There's no need to cry.'

'I know,' she choked out. 'I'm being s…silly.'

'Not silly at all,' he murmured. 'Just…over-tired. Time for you to get some proper sleep, I think. And time for me to go.'

Her head shot up off his chest. 'But you promised to stay the whole night!'

'I've changed my mind about that.'

'I don't want you to go,' she wailed.

'Don't worry. I'll be back,' he said, and firmly put her to one side whilst he sat up and swung his feet over the side of the bed.

She only just stopped herself from grabbing him to make him stay, but couldn't help asking, 'When? Tomorrow night?'

He sighed. 'I know I shouldn't but, yes, I promise to come back tomorrow night. Unless, of course, you've changed your mind about becoming my girlfriend for real,' he added, glancing over his shoulder at her. 'Then I could pick you up from your office, take you for drinks and dinner then back to my place for a very pleasant evening.'

Oh, how tempting it was to agree to his offer. So, why didn't she?

Because all the reasons why she'd rejected his original proposal were still there: he didn't love her. He would *never* love her. The fact that that re-alisation cut even deeper into her heart reinforced her decision to keep her affair with Ryan as short as possible. It worried her sick that she was already falling in love with him. How easy it would be to surrender to her emotional nature and just go along with whatever he wanted.

Don't do it, Laura, the bitter voice of experience insisted. *Stay strong!*

'I haven't changed my mind,' she said much more firmly than she felt.

'Fine,' he bit out as he climbed off the bed and

reached for his clothes. 'But don't go thinking you can have it all your way indefinitely, Laura. I'm not happy with this arrangement. Not happy at all.'

'Really?' she couldn't resist saying. 'I would have thought it was right up your alley—all fun and no responsibility.'

The look he gave her would have frozen mercury.

Laura might have panicked if it had lasted. But slowly the ice in his eyes thawed and a sardonic smile lifted one corner of his mouth. 'I can see you would have been one hell of a criminal-defence lawyer. You really are wasted in corporate law. Which reminds me, don't forget to tell them at work that I'm no longer your client and that they'll need to send me someone else.'

Dismay curled her stomach. 'But what excuse will I give them?'

Now his smile turned a little cruel. 'That's your problem, Laura.'

CHAPTER TWENTY-FOUR

'No!' Alison exclaimed in shocked tones for the umpteenth time.

Laura suppressed a sigh. Lord only knew how her friend would react if she told her the whole truth about her ongoing affair with Ryan. She'd actually contemplated lying when Alison had rung her first thing this morning, barely five minutes after she arrived at work. But in the end she'd decided that a sanitised version of the truth would still save her pride, at the same time satisfying Alison's by-then rabid curiosity.

So she'd confessed to having sex with Ryan again when they'd returned to Sydney yesterday, but made it sound like it had been her idea that he eventually go home rather than stay the night. But when she confessed that she'd refused to become his girlfriend for real, opting instead for a brief sexual fling, Alison's reaction had still been negative.

'And you honestly think you can handle a strictly

sexual affair?' Alison went on eventually in a calmer vein. 'That might suit lover boy but it's not you, Laura.'

Laura refused to let her friend think Ryan was to blame for everything. 'Try not to forget, Alison, that I've been a willing partner in all this. I want sex from Ryan as much as he wants it from me.'

'He must be damned good in bed to get you into this state. You've never cared for sex all that much in the past, not even when you were madly in love. But, of course, he *has* had a lot of experience,' she added tartly.

'Yes,' Laura agreed, wondering if Alison could be just a tad jealous. She was always saying that one's sex life went out the window when you had children.

Alison sighed. 'You know, I envy you, in a weird kind of way,' she admitted, confirming Laura's thoughts.

'Not as much as I envy you,' Laura retaliated. 'I'd give anything to have a loving husband like your Peter and two gorgeous children. You have a fantastic family, Alison.'

'I guess I do. It's just that… Oh, never mind. Look, don't take any notice of me today. I'm suffering from PMT; you know what it's like.'

'Indeed I do.' Laura frowned as she realised that she didn't have any of the symptoms yet.

Feeling slightly panicky, she went over the dates in her head again and came up with the same result—her period was definitely due on Wednesday. It occurred to her that maybe PMT went away when you were having a fantastic sex life. Maybe her body had become more relaxed. Stress could do dreadful things to one's health. Or so she'd read.

'What you need to do,' she told Alison, 'Is to have more sex.'

'Huh! And when exactly do I have time for sex? Those gorgeous kids of mine run me ragged.'

'Make time, Alison. I'll mind your kids next weekend and you go away with Peter.'

'Honestly? You'd do that?'

'I've minded them before.'

'Not for a whole weekend. You know, I think that's a great idea and I will take you up on it— eventually. But not this weekend. There's no point; I'll have my period.'

'You and me both,' Laura said dryly. 'Look, I have to go, Alison. I have heaps of work to do.'

Which was not strictly true. But she had to think up some plausible reason why she could no longer be Ryan's lawyer. It was sure to be the first thing he would ask her that evening.

But, as it turned out, Laura couldn't think of a reason—not one she felt happy with. Already she was feeling hyped up about tonight. Hyped up and turned on. Thoughts of sex filled her head all day, so much so that by the time Ryan arrived on her doorstep shortly after seven she'd forgotten all about not having organised another lawyer. All she could think of was being with him. One look at his hotly glittering eyes and she knew he felt exactly the same.

They made it into the bedroom, but not the bed. And Ryan almost didn't use a condom—again! She was the one who reminded him just in time. When he swore, she laughed. Then he laughed. The delay was exactly what they needed to catch their breath and move from the hard wooden floor to the comfort of the bed. They even managed to remove their clothes before a burst of uncontrollable passion overtook them again.

Laura came the moment Ryan entered her, his own climax swiftly following. After his body stopped shuddering he collapsed across her, his weight almost crushing. When she pushed at his shoulders, he levered himself up onto his elbows and glared down at her.

'I can't keep this up, you know,' he growled.

Her brain felt as glazed as her eyes. 'Keep what up?'

'Waiting all day to be with you. I nearly went insane this afternoon.'

'Oh…'

'Is that all you've got to say? *Oh*?'

'I don't know what you want me to say.'

'Say that you feel the same way. Say you'll stop this nonsense and agree to be my girlfriend for real. Then we could spend lunchtimes together and have proper dates. And weekends away.'

Again, she was tempted to agree. But the bottom line was that he still only wanted her for sex with some company thrown in. There would be no proposal of marriage at any stage.

She said the only thing that she knew would stop him in his tracks. 'If I become your girlfriend for real, Ryan, I'm sure to fall in love with you.'

Ryan could not believe the crazy thoughts which ran through his head—mostly that he didn't care any more if she fell in love with him as long as she let him spend more time with her.

God, how selfish could he get?

Ryan rolled away from her, staring grimly up at the ceiling and wondering what the hell he should do. He didn't like it that he was becoming possessive of her. It worried him.

Laura could not believe how forlorn she felt when he abandoned her body. Forlorn and alone. He was lying right beside her yet he seemed such a long way away. She hated that feeling.

'I'm sorry,' she said suddenly, not really knowing what she was apologising for.

He turned his head to look at her. 'For what? Being honest? I like honest people. And I like you—very much so.'

'I…I like you too,' she said, choking on the words as she realised what an understatement they were. Because, of course, she didn't just *like* him any more. She *loved* the man. It wasn't the thought of no more sex with him that terrified the life out of her but of never seeing him again.

It was a shattering realisation. Laura quickly turned her head away lest her face betray the truth.

'I doubt you'd fall in love with me, Laura,' he said at that most ironic moment. 'By the way, what did you tell your boss about why you couldn't be my lawyer any more?'

Laura cleared her throat. 'I…er…haven't told him yet.'

'Then don't.'

Her head whipped round to stare at him. 'But why?'

'I don't want another lawyer. I want you.'

'What about your rule about sleeping with work colleagues?'

He shrugged. 'Rules are meant to be broken.'

His nonchalance infuriated her, especially after all the fuss he'd made. 'You can break *your* rule,' she snapped, 'But I have no intention of breaking mine. You're my client now and I do not have relationships with clients.'

He speared her with cold blue eyes. 'But you don't have a relationship with me, Laura. You're just having sex with me. Which reminds me, I take it you don't want to call it quits tonight either, do you? You want me to come back tomorrow night as well.'

Laura's teeth clamped down hard. He was deliberately trying to goad her. But she refused to be goaded. 'I guess that's up to you, Ryan. I can't force you to come.'

'But you want me to.'

She lifted her chin in a defiant manner. 'Yes,' she bit out.

'In that case, I'll be here tomorrow night. But after that I suggest we have a week's break from each other. That should stop us growing too attached.'

She wanted to hate him at that moment.

'What about our appointment on Friday afternoon?' she asked waspishly.

'The contracts can wait another week. Things are a bit slow at the moment. Now, I really must go to the bathroom. Meanwhile, I suggest you go get that bottle of white wine that I saw in your fridge door last night. I could do with a drink.'

'I was going to have that later with dinner,' she threw after him.

'Good God,' he said mockingly as he strode from the room. 'She's going to feed me as well. What a lucky fellow I am.'

Now she did hate him.

But not as much as Ryan hated himself. He scowled at his reflection in the bathroom mirror. What right did he have to say nasty things like that?

If you don't like the 'strictly sex' arrangement

Laura wants, then you should just keep on walking, right out of her life.

So why didn't he?

Be honest, you hypocritical bastard. It's just your pride lashing out. You really want to stay.

By the time Ryan finished washing his hands, he'd resolved to stop being stupid and just give Laura plenty of what she wanted. But he wanted to make love to her; that was the truth of it.

Ryan shook his head at himself in the mirror. It was as well that he'd suggested they have a break from each other; he was becoming way too involved. He also revised his idea about keeping her on as his lawyer. But he wouldn't tell her that just yet. He'd tell her tomorrow night.

CHAPTER TWENTY-FIVE

LAURA'S period didn't arrive on Wednesday morning, or Wednesday afternoon, or Wednesday evening. When Thursday morning came and still no sign of a period, her stress levels soared. Suddenly, she was thankful that she and Ryan were not in contact for a week. No phone calls, or text messages; no emails. Nothing until the following Tuesday when he'd be dropping round after work around seven.

The last time she'd seen him he'd said they both needed time to think, which was certainly true. Because by then she was more in love with him than ever, so much so that she was reconsidering accepting his offer of being his girlfriend for real and to hell with the consequences. She'd almost said as much when he had gone to leave. She might have done so if he hadn't opened his mouth to say he'd changed his mind about keeping her on as his lawyer.

'Don't worry about finding a replacement immediately,' he'd added. 'That can wait a while.'

It was a well-timed reminder that nothing had
changed for Ryan. Any secret fantasies she'd
been harbouring about his feelings for her having
deepened went out of the window. So, yes, she
definitely needed time to think about what she
was going to do when she saw him the following
Tuesday.

By Friday, Laura's period still hadn't made an
appearance. It was a huge relief that she wasn't in
contact with Ryan, because he might have asked
her about it. This way, she didn't have to explain
things. For Lord knew how he would react. He
might think she'd lied to him and had somehow
been trying to trap him with a pregnancy. As if
she would!

But she could not deny that strangely, as soon
as the thought entered Laura's head that she might
have somehow conceived Ryan's child, by some
perverse twist of fate, the idea of having his baby
brought a zing to her heart. But the zing did not
last, fading to a deep dismay when she realised it
would definitely mean the end of any relationship
with Ryan. Because he didn't do love or marriage
or, God forbid, fatherhood.

That night she actually prayed for her period to arrive. But her prayers were not answered, not for another few days. Perversely, she cried when it did arrive the following Tuesday morning—cried and cried and cried. She was so distressed that she rang work and said she would not be in. Several times that day, she picked up her phone to call Ryan and tell him she didn't want him to come over that night. But each time she put the phone back down again. Love made one weak, she accepted despairingly. And there she'd been, thinking she was over being a victim to love.

Laura thought about what she would say to Ryan all afternoon, determined not to let him come inside. She even began to hope that he might not come at all. But he showed up, looking impossibly handsome in a suit and tie. Her resolve faltered when he smiled at her— Faltered even more when he said, 'God, but I've missed you,' then pulled her into his arms.

She didn't object to his kiss, telling herself that this was her goodbye kiss. But, oh, inside she was already dissolving.

'I'm sorry, Ryan,' she said when he finally let her come up for air. 'But you have to stop. I…I've got my period.'

'Still?'

She looked into his eyes and saw surprise, not scepticism.

'No. It… It didn't arrive till today,' she admitted. Now he looked shocked. 'But you said…'

'I know what I said,' she swept on angrily, knowing exactly what he'd thought for a split second. 'I don't know what happened. I was so worried about being late that I actually went to a doctor yesterday and he told me that sometimes ovulation is delayed from stress. He asked me what had been going on in my life, and when I told him about Gran's accident he said that might have done it. Anyway, he said it was too early to test for a pregnancy but it wasn't impossible that I might have conceived. You can imagine how I felt at that moment!'

'No,' he said, looking oddly at her. 'How did you feel?'

It angered her even further, that coolly speculative look in his eyes.

All the distress of the last week welled up inside her, goading her tongue to strike out at him.

'How do you think I felt?' she snapped. 'You don't think that I wanted your baby, do you? Good God, I'd have to be insane to want that! It's bad enough that I let myself be seduced into a disgustingly futile affair with a man who offered me nothing of himself but his body—if it turned out I *was* pregnant, I think I would have jumped off the harbour bridge!'

'You don't mean that,' he ground out.

'I do indeed,' she returned fiercely, all reason abandoned with her loss of temper. 'What decent woman would want your baby? You'd make a terrible father. Why, you are the most selfish, self-centred, screwed-up man I've ever known! Even Mario was a better man than you. And that's saying something!'

He just stared at her for a long moment, his eyes haunted. And then he nodded. Slowly. Sadly. 'I couldn't have said it better myself,' he agreed.

The horror of her words finally sank in to Laura, bringing with it an almost unbearable shame. She had no right to hurt him like she just had. No right at all. As she'd said to Alison, she'd been a willing partner in all this. Besides, not wanting marriage and a family didn't make Ryan a bad person. He had every right to live his life as he saw fit, and it wasn't as though he hadn't been honest with her.

But it was too late now. The words had been said and she couldn't take them back. Though, heaven help her, she wanted to, wanted to throw herself back into his arms and beg him to forgive her. Instead, she took a shaky step backwards, her fingers curling over into fists by her side lest her arms moved without her brain telling them to.

'I do apologise if I have behaved badly,' he said bleakly. 'I honestly never meant to hurt you. I think you are an incredible woman and I'm sure that some day your Mr Right will come along and give you what you want. Please tell your family I'm sorry things didn't work out between us but I wish them well also, especially your gran.'

His mentioning her gran tipped Laura's emotions into dangerously weak territory.

'Ryan, I…'

'No, Laura,' he cut in, whipping up one hand as a quite savage stop sign. 'You've said quite enough. Let's leave it at that. Bye, Rambo,' he added when the cat suddenly appeared at his feet. 'Look after your mistress for me.' And, whirling, he was gone.

Laura stood in the open doorway, staring at the empty path for what felt like an eternity. This time her tears were silent, spilling over and running down her cheeks, dripping from the end of her nose onto her top. No doubt it was being ruined, yet she didn't care. Laura suspected she would not care about anything for a long time to come.

The sound of her phone ringing and ringing eventually forced her to turn and walk down the hallway towards the kitchen, a disconsolate Rambo trailing behind her. Probably a telemarketer, Laura thought wearily; they always rang when people got home from work. Sighing, she snatched a handful of tissues from the box which she kept on the counter, wiped her nose then reached for the phone.

'Yes?' she said in a decidedly dead voice.

'Oh—Laura,' Aunt Cynthia choked out down the line. 'Oh my dear…'

Laura's already breaking heart shattered into tiny pieces, for she knew immediately what had happened. And there she'd been, naïvely thinking nothing could possibly make her feel worse.

But she hadn't bargained on this.

Life wasn't just cruel she realised as her insides crumbled in despair—sometimes it was downright sadistic.

'What happened?' she asked in hollow tones. 'A heart attack, I suppose?'

'Yes, we think so. Jane had gone to lie down after lunch, as she always did. I went to wake her around five and she was just lying there, unconscious. We called the ambulance but there was nothing they could do. She was already dead by the time they arrived. She didn't suffer, Laura. She looked very…peaceful. Happy, even.'

'That's good,' was all Laura could manage to say, tears threatening once more.

'You know, I thought I wouldn't be this upset when she went,' her aunt said with a sob. 'But I can't seem to stop crying.'

Laura knew how she felt.

'I'll have to ring you back, Aunt Cynthia. I can't talk any more just now.'

Hanging up, she sank down on the floor, put her head in her hands and began to sob.

CHAPTER TWENTY-SIX

RYAN could not remember the drive back to the city; his mind was in total disarray. That he made it back to his apartment building without incident was a minor miracle. It was a struggle to concentrate on the road when his head was full of such distressing thoughts, the main one being that he would never see Laura again. Never hold her in his arms again. Never make love to her again. Even worse was the physical distress which accompanied these thoughts. His stomach was churning, and his chest muscles were so tight around his heart he imagined he might go into cardiac arrest at any moment.

As soon as he closed the door behind him, Ryan headed for his drinks cabinet and poured himself the largest straight whisky he'd ever had in his life, downing it quickly before pouring himself another. Before long, the alcohol did what his normally strong will could not, calmed his body and shut down his brain.

The following morning he rang his PA and told her he wouldn't be in for the rest of the week. Then he turned off his phone so that no one could bother him. For the next three days, he watched movie after movie, eating delivered pizzas and drinking himself into oblivion until he fell asleep in the lounge. Same thing on Saturday. By Sunday morning, he couldn't stand his own company any longer, or the way he looked when he happened to catch a glimpse of himself in the bathroom mirror.

A shower and a shave went some way to brightening him up, plus a litre of orange juice and a couple of aspirin for his hangover. Afterwards he went for a long walk around the nearby botanic gardens, during which time he thought and thought, mostly about the past, the kind of thinking Ryan was not well acquainted with. He put such activities in the same category as psychological analysis or, even worse, group-therapy sessions. He'd survived so far without the help of antidepressants and in-depth counselling, well aware that people in this modern day and age would think him something of a dinosaur regarding his attitude to mental health.

Ryan had no doubt that if he went to a doctor and confided the truth about his childhood he or she would be amazed that he'd lasted this long without cracking up entirely. His grandmother had actually taken him to a psychiatrist not long after his mother's death—or perhaps it was a psychologist; he couldn't be sure now, it was so long ago. But Ryan hadn't liked the man. He certainly hadn't wanted to tell him all the shameful details of his mother's life—and death—and hadn't wanted to keep reliving any of it.

He'd decided then and there to survive his own way. Of course, if it hadn't been for his grandmother's support and love, he would not have survived at all, let alone become a success. Ryan could also see that shortly after her death he'd been in real danger of losing it for a while. Only by hardening his heart even further against emotional attachment of any kind had he managed to continue living.

And it had worked for him up until now...

As Ryan walked endlessly around the garden pathways, he forced himself to face the astonishing fact that Laura had somehow stolen past his defences and melted his cold heart. His pretending that it was just lust he felt for her was just so much rubbish: it was love, pure and simple. Well, perhaps not so pure or so simple, but love all the same. Nothing else could explain the devastation he'd felt when she'd verbally savaged him the way she had the previous Tuesday.

But his falling in love with Laura was the ultimate irony, because she didn't return his love. Anyone could see that. Her disgust at the very thought of having his baby had been obvious. Though startled, deep down he'd actually not been displeased by the possibility—another light-bulb moment, if he'd been smart enough to recognise it at the time.

But he recognised it now.

By the time Ryan made it back to his apartment, he'd made a few decisions and got back some of his fighting spirit. Okay, so he probably didn't have a great chance of ever convincing Laura that he was a changed man. But he wasn't about to live the rest of his wretched life without giving it his best shot.

Winning a woman like Laura was not unlike winning a soccer match against a top team, he conceded. You couldn't just barge back into her life, running around like a chook with its head cut off. You had to have a decent strategy. A plan.

By Monday morning Ryan still wasn't sure what to do. He could hardly just ring Laura up and tell her that he loved her; that wasn't going to work. He needed more time to think. At the same time he needed to get back to work. Unfortunately, three days out of the office meant he had a lot of calls to return, one of them to Laura's boss.

'Ryan Armstrong,' he said when Greg Harvey came on the line.

'Ryan, so glad you called. I gather you'll be needing a new lawyer now that Laura has left us.'

'What? Laura's *left*?'

'You didn't know? I thought she would have told you. She resigned late last week. For personal reasons.'

'What kind of personal reasons?'

'I guess there's no reason you shouldn't know. Her grandmother died. Apparently they were very close.'

Ryan suppressed a groan of dismay.

'We offered her time off,' the man rattled on, 'But she said she needed a complete break. We're sorry to lose a lawyer of her ability but life does go on, doesn't it? Look, there's a young chap who's just joined us. Brilliant legal brain. What say I send him down to meet you, see what you think? His name's Cory Sanderland.'

'Sounds perfect, Greg. But not right now. I have

to go out shortly and I won't be in for the rest of the day. Leave it with me and I'll give Cory a call later this week.'

'Fine.'

'Have to go, Greg,' he said, and hung up.

But he didn't leave the office straight away. First he tried ringing Laura's mobile but it was turned off. After pacing around for a few minutes, he charged out to his PA's desk.

'Judith,' he said. 'I want you to contact Laura Ferrugia's PA and find out the phone number of Laura's best friend. Her name is Alison—that's all I know, I'm afraid. I know it's an odd request but just do this for me, will you?'

Judith, who was a sensible woman who liked her job, didn't argue. 'Fine.'

Five minutes later, she handed Ryan a piece of paper with a phone number written down on it.

'She didn't really want to give it to me,' she said. 'You didn't tell me that Laura no longer worked there. I had to say it was an emergency.'

'It *is* an emergency,' he told her.

'Care to tell me more?'

'Not right now.'

'Just as well I'm not a curious type,' she said, and went back to her desk.

He called the number straight away, his heartbeat quickening as he waited for someone to answer. At last, a woman's voice said, 'Hello?'

'Is that Alison?'

'Yes? Who is this?'

'Ryan Armstrong.'

He heard her sharp intake of breath. 'What on earth are you doing ringing *me*?'

'I just heard about Laura's grandmother,' he said swiftly. 'I've been trying to ring Laura but her phone's switched off. I was hoping you could tell me if her grandmother's been buried yet. I'd like to go to the funeral.'

'Laura wouldn't want you there.'

'I'd still like to go.'

'Oh, for pity's sake, give the girl a break, will you? And just stay away from her. She doesn't want any more to do with you.'

Ryan decided then and there that if he wanted to win Laura he also had to win her best friend.

'She doesn't want anything to do with the man I used to be,' Ryan said. 'She might want to have something to do with the man I am today.'

'And what's that, pray tell?'

No doubting the cynicism in her voice.

'A man in love.'

Now he heard an even sharper intake of breath.

'I love Laura, Alison. And I want to marry her. Now tell me when the funeral is.'

'Oh Lord, it's today. In a couple of hours.'

'And you're not there with her?' he threw at her somewhat accusingly.

'I would have been but my little boy isn't well. He's asthmatic, you see, and has a bad bout of hay fever today. I daren't leave him.'

'I see. Is it being held at the chapel near the Hunter Valley gardens?' he asked.

'Yes. How did you know?'

'Never mind. I have to go, Alison, if I'm going to make it in time.'

'Yes, yes. Just go. And Ryan?'

'Yes?'

'For what it's worth, I think Laura loves you too.'

A wild joy flooded Ryan's heart. 'What makes you think so?'

'I've thought so from the day after she went to bed with you. Laura only has sex with men she loves. She's that kind of girl.'

Ryan smiled. That was one of the reasons he loved her.

'Have to go, Alison.'

'Hurry, Ryan. Laura needs you.'

Yes, he agreed silently as he grabbed his suit jacket and headed for the door. Just as much as he needed her. They needed each other, two lonely, seriously screwed-up people whom life had hurt but whom life hadn't totally beaten yet.

Laura sat in the front pew of the chapel, trying not to look at her gran's coffin, or the masses of yellow roses which covered the lid. Every time she looked at the yellow roses she wanted to cry. They had been Jane's favourite flower. When Laura had left school and started living in her parents' house at North Manly, her gran had bought her several yellow rose-bushes to plant in her garden to remind Laura of her.

As if I would ever need reminding, Laura thought as tears threatened once more.

Panic joined her tears, for it was her turn to speak. Uncle Bill and Aunt Cynthia had asked her to give the main eulogy, claiming they were both poor public speakers whereas she was used to it. She'd shied away from doing it at first before accepting that it was the last way she would be able to express her gratitude to Jane for all she'd done for her. She'd written down what she wanted to say, lest she forget it. Now she stared down at the piece of paper on which she'd written the in-adequate words, seeing that it was nothing more than a twisted crunched-up mess in her lap. It was impossible to straighten it out.

When Aunt Cynthia nudged her in the ribs, she rose and stumbled up to the podium. Somehow she managed to relate the story of Jane's early life from memory, dry facts really, about where her grandmother was born and where she went to school. She spoke of Jane's love of country life and of gardening. She then mentioned her marriage, complimenting her on being a loving and loyal wife, and a devoted mother.

But the moment she came to where she wanted to say how wonderful a grandmother she had been, her mouth went bone dry and a huge lump filled her throat. She looked down and tried to straighten out the crumpled sheet of paper but it was all a blur. Dying of embarrassment, she was staring down the only aisle of the small church when suddenly, through the blur, striding towards her with forceful steps, was the last man on earth she expected to see at that moment. My God, she thought wildly as her heart whirled and her heart lurched. What on earth was Ryan doing here?

He didn't hesitate, crossing the strip of carpet

that still separated them, stepping up to stand close to her and slide a strongly supportive arm around her waist.

'Sorry I'm late,' he said gently as he pulled her against him. 'Got a bit lost without Jane's splendid directions.'

Laura blinked up at him, having been rendered even more speechless than before.

'I take it you're having a spot of trouble,' he whispered, having glanced down at the still-crinkled paper. 'As you can see, folks,' he continued in full voice, 'Laura is slightly overcome with the situation. Which is understandable, given how much she loved her gran. So I'm going to finish speaking for her. For those of you who don't know me, my name is Ryan Armstrong and I'm Laura's boyfriend.'

Ryan hoped like hell that she hadn't said anything to her family about their having broken up. He suspected that she might not have done so just yet. She was proud, his Laura. He felt reassured by Cynthia's eyes, which weren't looking at him with shock, or even surprise—reassured also by Laura's acquiescence to his arm around her.

'Now, I didn't know Jane all that well,' he went on. 'We only met once, over one short weekend.

But that was long enough for me to see she was one of those grandmothers that make the world a better place to live in, especially for their grandchildren. I know something about grandmothers like that. I had one myself. I know how Laura feels, and on her behalf I'd like to thank Jane, as well as all the other amazing grandmothers in this world, for their sweetly giving natures, their unconditional love and their wonderful wisdom.

'I'm sure if Jane could speak to us today, she would tell us all gathered here in her memory not to be sad. She would want us to celebrate her life, not mourn her death. I know she was extremely proud of Laura, and all her family. Bill, Cynthia, Shane and Lisa: she loved you all dearly.

'She was also proud of where she lived. She recently showed me the Hunter Valley Gardens, along with this very beautiful little church, saying this was where she wanted her funeral service to be held. Both Laura and I hoped that such an event would be many years in the future. But it was not to be. Let me just say that it was a privilege to know Jane. Goodbye, darling Gran. Rest in Peace.'

Ryan's arm tightened around Laura as he led her back to her seat, sobbing now, taking a guess that she'd been sitting next to her aunt and uncle in the front pew.

'Well said, Ryan,' Bill complimented, his own eyes shimmering with tears. Cynthia was incapable of saying anything, a handkerchief held up to her face as she wept quietly into it.

Ryan found himself quite choked up too, feeling genuine grief—and some more remorse too, for not flying back to Australia and speaking at his own grandmother's funeral. If only one could go back in time…

But he could still remember how alone he'd felt at the time, thinking that the one and only person in his life that he could count on was gone. Laura was probably feeling the same.

He had to make her see, however, that she *could* count on him, that he wasn't the feckless fool she imagined him to be. She was still weeping quietly when they left the church. Ryan was thankful that they weren't going on to some wretchedly dreary graveyard, Bill quickly explaining to him outside the church that his mother had requested that she be cremated privately and her ashes sprinkled on her beloved rose garden. It seemed a much better ending, in Ryan's opinion, than being buried. But each to his own.

'Where's the wake being held?' he asked Bill.

'Back at the house. I presume Laura will be going back in your car, Ryan?'

'Yes, of course.'

'See you back there shortly, then.'

When Ryan steered Laura over to where he'd parked his car, she didn't argue with him, a testimony to her distressed state. But shortly after they joined the long lines of cars heading back to the house she pulled herself together and glanced over at him with a deep frown crinkling her forehead.

'I still don't understand how you knew about Gran's funeral,' she said. 'Or even why you came.'

Ryan supposed he could make up a plausible lie—that he'd seen a funeral notice in the paper. But he didn't want to do that. He wanted to be totally honest with Laura from now on. It was the only way she would be able to trust him.

'Greg Harvey told me about your gran's death this morning when he rang to offer me a new lawyer. I tried to ring you straight away but your phone's turned off. So I rang Alison and she told me when and where the funeral was.'

'Alison? But you don't know her number.'

'I made it my business to find it.'

'But *why*?' There was total confusion in her voice.

'Because I love you, Laura,' he said, turning to look her straight in the eye.

Laura's mouth fell open, her eyes widening at the same time.

'I love you and I want to marry you,' he added, knowing that a declaration of love was not going to be enough. For how many men used false words of love to seduce women back into their beds? He had never been guilty of such tactics but he imagined other men had. Certainly dear old Mario and Brad had.

'You want to marry me?' she echoed, clearly in shock at his proposal.

'Yes. And have children with you. I want it all. I've been thinking about it for days and that's what I want with you, Laura. I'm hoping that's what you want too.'

Laura could hardly believe what she was hearing, or contain the joy that washed into her until then despairing soul. For she knew instinctively that Ryan would not lie about something as serious as marriage and children. Love, yes; he might lie about that. But not the rest.

It came to her suddenly that he must know about

her falling in love with him. Alison would have told him something. Dear, romantic-minded Alison who could not resist a happy ending, no matter how unlikely the couple.

'Did Alison tell you that I loved you?' she choked out.

'She said she thought you did,' he admitted. 'But I would have come today even if she hadn't said anything.'

Somehow, his knowing that she loved him momentarily burst her bubble of happiness. It brought doubts as well. Laura needed more understanding of his dramatic change of heart before she could blindly say yes to his amazing proposal. She needed the comfort of knowledge.

'But you said you would never fall in love, or get married and have children,' she pointed out.

'That was before I met you, Laura.'

'No, you said it *after* you met me. You said it more than once. You warned me.'

'I didn't realise then that I would fall in love with you. I didn't know what falling in love felt like. I didn't think I was capable of it.'

'But *why* would you think that? Everyone is capable of love.'

'I know that now. But till I met you I refused to let it into my life.'

'You have to tell me why, Ryan. You have to make me understand. I do love you, more than I ever thought possible. But I can't marry you unless I know why you felt like that.'

He sighed, then nodded. 'You're right; I know you're right. It's just so damned hard to talk about it, that's all.'

'If you truly love me, Ryan, then you have to trust me with your past. I promise I will never tell another living soul. Not Alison. Not anyone.'

Laura could see the difficulty he was still having, opening up to her. What terrible trauma had he endured as a child, she wondered, that would make him retreat from emotion as he had? She hated to think he might have been abused in some way, but what else could it be?

'I love you,' she repeated. 'I will always love you, no matter what you tell me.'

He still didn't speak so she just sat there and said nothing further. The long line of cars was making slow progress on their way back to the house, giving him enough time to decide whether to confide in her or not.

'My mother didn't die of cancer,' he said at last. 'She was murdered.'

Laura only just managed not to gasp in shock, for it was the last thing she was expecting.

'But not by any stranger,' he added in a rough, emotion-charged voice. 'By my father. Her *de facto* husband. The man she said she loved. The man who claimed *he* loved *her*, even as she lay battered to death at his feet.'

'Oh, Ryan...'

'I found her, you know, when I came home from school. Lying next to the kitchen table in a pool of blood.'

'Oh my God...'

'She'd cooked me a cake. It was still on the table. It was my twelfth birthday.'

Laura closed her eyes. Lord in heaven, no child should have to endure that. She'd thought she'd had it bad when her parents had been killed. But it had been an accident. They hadn't been murdered.

'He was sitting on the floor next to her, crying. I...I...'

When it was obvious he could not go on, Laura reached over and placed her hand gently over his, which was suddenly gripping the wheel like a drowning man holding on to a piece of flotsam.

'You don't have to tell me any more right now. I can see you had good reasons to reject love and marriage and fatherhood. We'll talk about it later.' *Much* later.

Ryan shook his head. 'No, I want to tell you now. I want you to understand. It had been going on for years—the violence. The beatings. Not me, just Mum. The only times he hit me were when I tried to protect her. Even then he would just push me aside. He was insanely jealous of her. Wouldn't let her go to work, wouldn't let her leave the house or have any more babies. When she became pregnant once—I think I was about seven—he accused her of having an affair, then he punched her in the stomach over and over till she miscarried.'

'Oh my God! That's appalling, Ryan. But didn't people know what was going on? Your neighbours? Your grandparents?'

'Domestic violence was very common where we lived. A lot of the men were unemployed. My father did work occasionally, but he was unreliable. He was a drunk, you see. We mostly lived on welfare, in a housing-commission place which should have been condemned.

'As for relatives, Dad refused to have anything to do with any relatives, especially Mum's. Though

I knew my Mum's mother was alive. Mum told me her name and where she lived and said if anything ever happened to her that I was to go to my grandmother's place. She even hid some money in a secret place which she called my escape money. Many times I thought about taking it and just going, but how could I leave her to him? I begged her to come with me but she wouldn't. She said she loved him. I could never understand that. It made no sense to me.'

'I don't think she loved him at all by then, Ryan. She was simply scared to death of him. I had a battered wife as a client once. She stabbed her husband in the end.'

'I thought about killing my father several times. I wish I had.'

'I can imagine. So what happened to him? I presume he was arrested for murder?'

'He pleaded guilty and got twenty years. But he was bashed to death a few months later in jail. It seems the other prisoners don't take kindly to wife killers.'

'I can understand that. And I can understand you now, Ryan.' Very much so, the poor darling. It was no wonder he never wanted to talk about the past, and no wonder he'd rejected love for so long. 'I really appreciate your confiding in me, but you know what? I think we've done enough talking about the past for today. I would much prefer to talk about the future.'

He glanced over at her and smiled. 'A woman after my own heart.'

'Oh yes,' she said, smiling back at him. 'I *am* after your heart.'

'You already have it, my love.'

Her own heart turned over. 'I'm still coming to terms with that.'

'You're not the only one. When I realised I loved you, I wasn't sure what to do because I thought you would never love me back. I mean, how could you possibly love such a selfish, self-centred, screwed-up individual like me?'

Laura groaned. 'I hated myself afterwards for saying that, because I don't think that at all. I think you're a fine man, decent and kind, with a warm, loving soul. Look at the way you talked about grandmothers at the service just now. It was beautiful, the words you said.'

Ryan's heart squeezed tight at her sweet compliments. 'Can I take it, then, that you *will* marry me?'

Her eyes shone as she looked over at him. 'Whenever and wherever you would like.'

'How about first thing in the New Year, up here in Jane's favourite chapel?'

Laura smiled. 'Sounds like a good idea to me.'

EPILOGUE

'I CHRISTEN you Marisa Jane Alison Armstrong,' the minister said, the same minister who'd pronounced Ryan and Laura man and wife eleven months earlier in the same church.

'She was so good,' Alison complimented Laura when she handed the baby back after the ceremony. 'Not a peep out of her, not even when the holy water was poured over her forehead.'

'She loves water,' Ryan said proudly. 'I've got her booked in for swimming lessons when she turns six months.'

Alison and Laura exchanged amused glances.

'And when is she going to start playing soccer?' Alison's husband asked with a twinkle in his eye.

'Never too soon, Pete,' Ryan replied. 'Four or five is a good age. That way she can be a striker and not a boring old goalkeeper.'

'A striker,' Laura murmured, rolling her eyes and shaking her head. She still found it hard to believe just what a besotted father Ryan had become. As soon as he had found out she was pregnant, he'd turned into a real mother hen. When she'd suffered from morning sickness during her early weeks, he'd insisted she stop applying for new jobs and take it easy at home, a move which hadn't entirely displeased her; her own priorities had changed by then. But *she'd* insisted she at least remain *his* lawyer, to keep her hand in. She loved coming to his office every Friday afternoon at three p.m., though nowadays she was dressed a little more stylishly. Sometimes they didn't get much work done.

'Everyone back to the house for drinks,' Cynthia chimed in.

'Everyone' was not a large group, the only guests at the christening being Alison and Peter, along with Lisa and Shane, Bill and Cynthia. Their wedding had been a much larger affair with lots of Ryan's old friends and clients attending, followed by a slap-up reception at a local five-star resort.

But they'd decided to keep the christening much more private and personal. Alison's two children were being minded by their grandparents for a couple of days, giving Alison and Peter the opportunity for that romantic getaway that they had been meaning to have all year and not got around to. Ryan had booked them into the same five-star resort they'd spent *their* wedding night in—his treat, he insisted. The four of them had become close friends during the last year, with Ryan liking Peter's easy-going nature a great deal.

'I suggest you follow me,' Ryan told Peter as they made their way to where their cars were parked. 'It can be a bit tricky finding Bill and Cynthia's place. I'll drive slowly so you won't have any trouble keeping up.'

Ryan still took his time loading their precious cargo into the carry-cot in the back of his new family-friendly car, a four-door Lexus which he'd bought a few months back. His willingness to trade in his much-loved BMW had displayed to Laura more than anything he said just how much it meant to him to become a father. And how serious he was taking the role.

'They're a nice couple,' Ryan said when they were finally on their way. 'But their kids can be murder. I feel sorry for their grandparents.'

'Sibling rivalry,' Laura said, thinking of how she'd been with Shane, who'd been a kind of sibling to her.

'Spoilt, more like it,' Ryan said dryly. 'Have you seen how many toys they've got?'

'I don't think you can talk,' Laura pointed out. 'I can see already that you're going to give Marisa everything her little heart desires.'

'Oh, no I won't. She's going to learn the value of money. And of hard work.'

Laura groaned. 'You're not going to be one of those fathers, are you?'

'And what kind is that, madam?'

'Pushy. And bossy. And controlling.'

'Absolutely not! I hate controlling people.'

Laura laughed, then so did Ryan. 'You're right. I am a bit controlling. But I can change. I've changed a lot already.'

'You have indeed,' Laura said with warmth and love in her voice.

Ryan glanced over at his beautiful wife and smiled. 'I have one suggestion to make which might eliminate my spoiling our little princess back there.'

'Do tell.'

'We could have another baby.'

'So soon?'

'Why wait? Life is short, Laura.'

For a split second, Laura thought of her gran. And then she nodded. 'You're right. Another baby would be a good idea.'

'All my ideas are good.'

'Oh Ryan,' she said with a soft laugh. 'You are incorrigibly arrogant. But that's all right. I love you just the same.'

'That is why I love *you* so much, my darling.'

'Oh?'

'Because you love me just the same.'

* * * * *

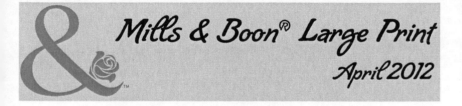

Mills & Boon® Large Print
April 2012

JEWEL IN HIS CROWN
Lynne Graham

THE MAN EVERY WOMAN WANTS
Miranda Lee

ONCE A FERRARA WIFE...
Sarah Morgan

NOT FIT FOR A KING?
Jane Porter

SNOWBOUND WITH HER HERO
Rebecca Winters

FLIRTING WITH ITALIAN
Liz Fielding

FIREFIGHTER UNDER THE MISTLETOE
Melissa McClone

**THE TYCOON WHO
HEALED HER HEART**
Melissa James

Mills & Boon® Large Print
May 2012

THE MAN WHO RISKED IT ALL
Michelle Reid

THE SHEIKH'S UNDOING
Sharon Kendrick

THE END OF HER INNOCENCE
Sara Craven

THE TALK OF HOLLYWOOD
Carole Mortimer

MASTER OF THE OUTBACK
Margaret Way

THEIR MIRACLE TWINS
Nikki Logan

RUNAWAY BRIDE
Barbara Hannay

WE'LL ALWAYS HAVE PARIS
Jessica Hart

0412 Rom LP

Mills & Boon® Online

Discover more romance at
www.millsandboon.co.uk

- **FREE** online reads
- **Books** up to one month before shops
- **Browse our books** before you buy

...and much more!

For exclusive competitions and instant updates:

 Like us on **facebook.com/romancehq**

 Follow us on **twitter.com/millsandboonuk**

 Join us on **community.millsandboon.co.uk**

Visit us Online | Sign up for our FREE eNewsletter at **www.millsandboon.co.uk**